W9-AUF-864

To John Wofford Dillard —
Thanks for everything
over the years.
Charles Wilkinson
7-20-07

CHARLES WILKINSON

GHOST OF A CHANCE

A NOVEL

Cold Tree Press
Nashville, Tennessee

One section of this novel,
in a different but recognizeable form, was previously published in
Memphis Magazine.

Library of Congress Control Number: 2007928907

Published by Cold Tree Press
Nashville, Tennessee
www.coldtreepress.com

Printed in the United States of America
ISBN 978-1-58385-160-9

To John Wilson Spence, III

CHARLES WILKINSON

GHOST OF A CHANCE

A NOVEL

PART 1
A
A

Spring, 1992

After his wife left and started talking to a lawyer, Taylor Robinson could drive in peace from Memphis to his favorite Mississippi casino and play as long as he wanted. He had taken a proprietary interest in a certain seat at a certain blackjack table, and the same dealer each night pitched him cards with her manicured, practiced hands. Now and then he looked up into Ramona's stoney gaze. *Repo* Ramona, who had earned her moniker by taking back what little she gave, was a Las Vegas transplant, come to these backwaters as the riverboat casinos grew like the cotton that had previously been the only cash crop in the region. Generally a house dealer, Ramona relentlessly swept the players' chips off the table and put them into her rack with a slap of finality. Lately, though, Taylor had been getting some cards.

She was about Taylor's age, somewhere around forty, and nearly pretty: her face had a wholesome quality which didn't mix well with her tough broad demeanor. Sometimes, when Taylor was looking at his cards, he sensed her watching him. He would glance up and meet her vivid green eyes. There would be nothing at all in her gaze, but always, just before she looked away, he would think she was about to communicate something. It never amounted to more than a shrug.

He thought it had something to do with the cards. Counters are not hard to identify, and whether or not they are allowed to play depends pretty much on whether they are winning or losing. He figured she just wanted to let him know she was watching him. He had run into dealers before who, for whatever reason, acted as if the casino's money was their own and who wildly exaggerated the advantage counting conferred.

Late one night, he was winning and feeling expansive. She dealt him eleven; he doubled his bet with another black chip.

"Give it to me, love," he said.

She dealt him a ten and said, "Baby, it's all yours."

He looked up and saw color rising in her cheeks. Suddenly, something which had seemed improbable became obvious. While the other players around the table hooted drunkenly over their cards he asked softly, "Say, Ramona, are you married?" He had noticed that the wedding ring had come off her finger weeks before.

"I'm getting a divorce," she said.

"Really? I am too. We should go out and commiserate."

She smiled a smile that negated itself, turned into a parody. "You mean get together and trash the jerks?"

"Yeah, sure. Give me your number."

"No, I don't give out my number. You give me yours."

Three or four days passed before he came home to a message on his machine. "Taylor, this is Ramona. I'll call again tomorrow about six. Bye bye." He listened to the message three times, trying to hear anything at all in her tone. There was nothing there, no attempt to sound attractive, nothing. The message was just information.

He made it a point to be home the next evening. As he waited for her call, he realized how lonely he was. He wondered if he could stand another night alone in the futon he used for a bed. The phone rang promptly at six. "So where do you live?" he asked. She gave him the directions. She too lived in Memphis, because the casinos in Tunica County, some twenty miles from town, had not yet spawned the apartment complexes and subdivisions that would soon grow around them. "And what apartment number?"

"Just stop outside and honk," she said. "I'll hear you and come down." She didn't want him to know where her apartment was.

That night they went to dinner. Throughout the meal he could hear the sound of his own voice as he tried to make small talk, could hear himself chewing, hear the clink of the silver fork against his china plate. In response to his questions, she offered the bare minimum of information. He managed to find out that she had been raised in Las Vegas, where her father was in the casino business, and she had worked in casinos in one capacity or another ever since graduating from high school.

"Did you . . ."

She interrupted: "Me? No . . . just high school." She looked at him defensively. "My parents couldn't send me to college like yours did."

"How do you know I went to college?"

"Because what you do for a living is on the computer at the casino. You can't *teach* college without going there." Taylor found it interesting that they had yet to update this piece of misinformation, but he said nothing.

Ramona had come to Mississippi because her husband, now in parts unknown, had been unable to get a dealing job in Vegas. "Now he's gone, and I'm here for no good reason." She conveyed this information looking straight down at her plate, but every now and then she would meet his eyes, and for a moment the fugitive thing he had seen at the blackjack table would flit across her gaze like a shadow, and then be gone. He would find himself looking into something decorative and blank. Dinner stretched beyond the play to which he had planned to take her.

"You know, you can be a major distraction when I'm at the table."

"You're counting the cards, right?"

He hesitated. "I don't know if I'm talking to Ramona my sweetie or Ramona the dealer . . . in league with the casino."

She looked at her plate in silence for a long moment, as if she didn't care for either category, and Taylor felt his stomach tighten as he waited for her reply. Then she looked up: "Maybe who you are on the computer is a lie. Maybe *you* work for the casino."

"Huh?"

"Well, you're always there."

He hardly knew how to respond to this and began to eat again in silence as waves of suspicion washed over him. As he struggled for a new subject, their divorces occurred to him. "So, how did your split up come about?"

"We didn't get along . . . he left."

"And was it painful?"

She shrugged. "For him, maybe."

"But not for you?"

Her eyes flashed and he felt her bristle from across the table. "Why do you want to know that?"

"I don't know . . . just sometimes it's good to talk about things."

"Some things are better not discussed."

"Ramona, there's no need to be so"— Taylor struggled for the words— "closed, so defensive."

She glared at him. He looked down at the expensive filet getting cold on his plate as silence stretched out like a bad run of cards. "So what's growing up in Las Vegas like?" he asked.

When he took her home he dropped her off in the parking lot. She got out of the car quickly without looking at him. He expected never to see her again outside of the casino. But just before the door shut, he heard her say, "Let's do this again."

He replied automatically, "Next week?"

"Yeah. That would be okay."

"I'll see you at the casino and we'll firm it up. Or I'll call you . . . but what's your number?"

She pulled a notepad out of her purse and wrote it down, handed it to him through the window, and walked away without a word.

Taylor's playing partner tapped out in Vegas. The Reverend had taken a flight out a week before to play where a few of the smaller casinos offered better odds than anything in Tunica, specifically, the surrender option, in which the player can concede defeat after looking at his first two cards and only lose half his bet. For a card counter, it is the most valuable of any blackjack option, and Taylor had been looking forward to the results. But the Reverend called and said he needed a ticket back to Memphis—he had cashed in his return ticket as a last ditch effort—and at the Memphis airport he still looked stunned. "What happened?" Taylor asked. "I thought Vegas and surrender was your ticket to a better world."

"Faith is our ticket, my son."

"Of course, Reverend. But what happened?"

"No luck, my man, no luck at all," the Reverend said. "It should have worked. But I never got any cards. Having to surrender every other hand just prolonged the agony."

"How much did you take with you?"

"My whole stake."

Taylor felt disbelief rising. "You lost nine thousand dollars?" They had just teamed up and now his partner had lost his stake. "What's next?" Taylor asked.

"Well, I have a little problem regarding the next couple of weeks. Vegas got my money, but I got something from Vegas."

"What?"

"A young woman. God brought us together over a crap table at Caesar's. She's coming here the day after tomorrow. I think she's either a high roller herself or used to hanging around them, for sure—her mother lives in Vegas and her father in Palm Springs. Naturally, she doesn't know I tapped out, and I don't even have the money to buy her a meal."

Taylor was seething. "What were you doing at the crap table?"

"Trying my luck. I wasn't having any at blackjack."

The moment the Reverend got up from the blackjack table and went to the crap table he went from having a tiny advantage—if he was counting the cards as Taylor had taught him—to a disadvantage. At that point, he was just another fool gambler.

"I'll stake you, Reverend," Taylor said. "But don't ever let me hear about you around a crap table again."

"Stormy says she nearly always wins. She's got a system."

Stormy. A system, yet. A system at the crap table was nothing more than systematic wild guessing. When Taylor first started playing seriously and his former friends would ask, with a raised eyebrow and a knowing tone, whether his blackjack "system" was still working, he would attempt to explain that what a card counter did had nothing to do with a "system," as it were—but he finally realized they weren't listening. They didn't want him to win. They were waiting for the big fall, when they could snicker and congratulate each other on their good sense for not being taken in like Taylor.

"This girl a stripper? A working girl?"

"Far as I know she's just a player."

Well, she had that in her favor. Taylor would take a player anytime. Even a fool crap player would have faith, hope, and imagination. Some gamblers did have sense. Nine out of ten, though, were idiots, and it seemed the Reverend had joined them.

"How much do you need?"

"Well, I've got a complimentary place down on the coast at the MGM Grand—chummed up with a supervisor at the Vegas Grand. It was the least he could do for a man of the cloth as down on his luck as I was." The Reverend touched his mail-order white collar. "For whenever I want it. Stormy wants to see the Gulf of Mexico. When she gets into town, we'll drive down there and play for a few days before we come back here. Then the three of us will play the next couple of weeks at Tunica."

"Once again, Reverend, how much do you need?" He was Taylor's partner, after all, and even though he had gone to Vegas on his own they generally pooled their money. Of course, they also generally played together, pushing the dealer from first and third positions on the blackjack table, and they did not play craps. They did not play craps, slots, roulette, baccarat, Let It Ride, Caribbean stud, or any other shyster game the casinos offered. They played blackjack.

"Just a couple of grand—to make sure I don't tap out."

"I guess you're trying to impress this girl with what a high roller you are."

"I need a decent stake to get my money back. He that hath much will be given more."

Taylor had been on a losing streak himself lately, and two grand wasn't pocket change. But the Reverend had a point. He wasn't going to get his money back betting nickels. "You just keep away from the crap table, and don't get steamed, and don't raise your bet when the count doesn't warrant it. You're playing with my money now, and you better play like a goddamned machine."

"I know how to play blackjack, and the Lord surely won't bless you with luck if you take His name in vain," the Reverend said, looking at Taylor beneficently, his face beaming above the frayed collar that had already changed from white to beige and was in the process of becoming a solid brown. He wore his filthy vestments when the occasion presented itself because, as he had said on more than one occasion, "A man of the cloth is granted certain privileges."

Taylor's wife came back into the picture. She was a tallish redhead in a business suit, body and soul, with a no-nonsense demeanor—at least she had at some point become the person resembling this description, which was not the woman he remembered marrying—but even their chastest hugs still felt good to Taylor. There was a lot to be said for simply feeling comfortable with someone. For the moment, there was some question as to whether or not she had actually had her lawyer file the divorce papers (she was cagey on this subject); she still loved him, etc. A part of Taylor wanted to save his marriage; part of him knew that his gambling and her response to it had created an irrevocable situation. On the third or fourth night that she had come to the little apartment he had rented after their separation, he asked, "So, Sarah, are we getting back together?"

"We need to give it some time," she said.

"How much?"

"I was thinking about a year. I need to know that this gambling has stopped."

She had been kept in the dark about his recent activities. "A year?" Taylor looked at her colorless fingernails, bitten to the quick, as she bent down, nodded, and scratched her practical flat-clad foot. A year. He looked beyond her at his apartment, shabby as it was, and thought about the house they were in the process of losing; Sarah would not pay her half of the mortgage. She wanted to sell it and he could not make the payments alone. She had never liked living in the country. The farmhouse on five acres. His dream. She didn't give a damn about his dreams.

Ramona's nails were long and red, she wore heels, and she didn't object to gambling.

Taylor and Ramona were to meet his friends at a French restaurant. Literary types in their forties, Thomas was an old friend of Taylor's, the woman someone he had never met, the most recent in a long succession of women the uncommitable Thomas was dating.

"So what does this Lillian do?" Ramona asked as they drove toward the restaurant.

Taylor had been given a brief overview, to which he had half-listened, knowing that she would soon be history. "I'm not sure. I think she's some kind of writer."

"Great," Ramona said. "I'll have a lot to say."

"You'll do fine," Taylor replied.

As they stood in the lobby and Taylor's eyes adjusted to the candlelight, Thomas and Lillian came into view at a corner table, waving them over. After the introductions, at which Lillian made an immediate impression on Taylor of intelligence and charm, she began asking Ramona questions which made Taylor wince inwardly. He already knew how Ramona would answer. He stared fixedly at the Clinton for President pin that Thomas had on his shirt, considered bringing up politics as a diversion, but couldn't force himself to do so in order to ward off the following:

"Where are you from, Ramona?

"I grew up in Vegas."

"Oh, I didn't know anyone was *from* Las Vegas."

Ramona said nothing.

"And you work in Tunica?"

"That's right."

"Are you a dealer?"

"Yes."

"Do you like it?"

"It's okay."

Lillian waited for Ramona to go on. Silence stretched and Taylor watched out of the corner of his eye as Ramona began to nibble steadily on a bread stick. He felt a kind of perverse admiration for the absolute shell she had constructed around herself. She didn't *give* away anything.

After this exchange, Lillian obviously found it easier to talk to the men, and began holding forth about her romantic experiences on the internet. This was a subject of some interest to Taylor, since he spent most of his days when he needed a break from the tables playing on the computer. The virtual reality game on which he played didn't have the new graphics; the "sets" were verbal descriptions. Still, it didn't take but a minute for a willing suspension of disbelief to establish itself, and a player left real life far behind.

"You're the only person I've talked to in person," Lillian said, "who understands the appeal of it. It's a new form of communication. Collaborative fantasy."

"I don't know how new that is," Thomas said cynically. "Sounds like love to me."

"Yes, and speaking of, I have a friend who met a guy from New Jersey online," Lillian said. "You know, we grew up in hippie days, in the free-love era when you'd meet, hop into bed, and then maybe get to know each other. But this was like an old-fashioned romance, a slow unveiling. Every day they would e-mail each other, and then eventually made plans to meet. Then they travelled back and forth. And a couple of weeks ago they got married."

Taylor wondered how "meeting and hopping into bed" sounded to Ramona, whom he suspected would never have been trusting enough to let down her guard or be spontaneous in that area. He glanced at her, and saw that she was merely looking at Lillian with a noncommittal expression.

"But I get on there just to play," Lillian continued. "There's nothing like it. I can be anybody I want to be"—she interrupted herself with a sardonic laugh—"which is sometimes an eighteen-year-old blond, none too bright, with a tattoo on my butt."

"I'll look for you, love," Taylor said, also laughing. "Or you can look for me. I play on one called *Stargate.* It's free and it's fun. A nice little virtual world." Ramona gave him a quick glance of mock anger—why did he want to see Lillian in the virtual world?—and Taylor felt a little flattered. At the same time, he wondered what Lillian was thinking . . . did Ramona sitting beside him with her tough casino vibe make him look good or bad in Lillian's eyes? And why did he care?

"I used to get online and sit in the corner and watch," Lillian said. "Then I started learning how to get noticed . . . in the first place, it's all in the name you choose."

Thomas, something of a technophile, mentioned that the technology to see and hear one another was already in the works in the form of "web-cameras." Both Taylor and Lillian said at the same time, "No, no, that would ruin it." Lillian added, "The whole appeal of it is the fantasy"—

"That and the anonymity," Taylor said. "Where no one knows you, you can be who you want to be."

"And sometimes you want to be *worse* than you've ever really allowed yourself to be," Lillian said. "Today I let a man get completely naked, excused myself to the bathroom, and slipped out the window." Taylor and Robert laughed. Ramona was silent but leaned forward, apparently listening intently. Lillian shook her head: "There was a long pause before I got the next message, I can tell you that, and when I did it was unrepeatable . . . you know, at work I spend my time writing ad copy for teenage girls, and I've gotten the hang of sounding like one, which can be fun whether you're slipping out a bathroom window or, like, just slippery."

At this point, with a self-deprecating tone, Ramona said softly, "I could write like a teenager." Thomas and Lillian looked at her in silence and Taylor gave her a quick hug . . . what did it matter?

Lillian still had everyone's attention, and the conversation turned autobiographical. She had lived in London, spent a couple of years studying painting in Taiwan, been chased all over Italy by Lotharios. "I couldn't walk down the street in Italy without getting a proposal," she said. "The Italians would say anything. Promise the world. But at one point I ran into a decent guy. He was telling me he was going to take me to London, and when he saw that I believed him he stopped and said, "Wait a minute. You don't actually believe this, do you?" I didn't know what to say. 'No, no,' he said, 'we Italian men just talk. You shouldn't believe a word we say. It's just a fantasy.' So I learned just to enjoy their company and not take what they said seriously."

Lillian's expression turned pensive and Taylor had the feeling he was about to hear something other than dinner party banter. "You know," she said. "I was thinking about that guy today and how I've used what he said at various times... It's strange how much influence someone you meet only once can have on your life."

Taylor and Ramona had to leave first in order to get to a movie. As they said goodbye, Taylor reminded Lillian where she could find him: "*Stargate*," he said. "I don't know if my name is memorable enough to get me noticed, but I never seem to have too much trouble. It's TRob Faulk."

"That might be just a little pretentious," Lillian said with a good-natured laugh.

"Maybe. But we reveal ourselves with our disguises and our heroes. What's your user-name?

"You'll know me if I show up."

Taylor flourished an imaginary hat, shook hands with Thomas, and he and Ramona took their leave.

Outside, Ramona smiled and made a gesture with her hand, rapidly touching her thumb and fingers, indicating Lillian's conversation. Taylor expected Ramona to be contemptuous of her, because she had so obviously had his attention while Ramona sat silently. He was afraid that the evening had fulfilled her worst expectations: boring intellectuals blathering . . . and he was also worried that the talk about the Internet might have seemed strange, maybe even sick, the perverted amusement of eggheads. But Ramona laughed and said, "She was funny. And she talked so much I didn't have to say anything." An expression of relief passed across her face, and she added, "I admire people like her, people who have been places and done things." Taylor sensed a generosity of spirit where he had nearly expected pettiness—which he would not have put beneath himself in a similar situation. Suddenly, he liked her very much.

On the way to the movie, he sensed something bothering her. He drove to a private lake in a residential section in the heart of the city. He knew a place where he could park close to the lake, see it through blossoming magnolias, and not be hassled by the homeowners or the police. The full moon's reflection floated in the driver's side view mirror. For some reason, he thought of the first time he and his wife had made love. Could it really be that they would put all that behind them? His attention was brought back by the palpable silence from the passenger seat.

"What's the matter?" he said.

"Nothing."

"Why do I feel like there's something bothering you ?"

"I don't know . . . you said I was 'hard and closed.' Well, you're right. I am closed up. I can't care about anybody right now, especially someone who's married. By the way, when's the last time you saw your wife?" Taylor started to lie and she cut him off. "Really, what I want to do is go home. Tell you what, take me home and next week you come to my place. I'll cook you dinner. But right now, I want to go home. . . and don't start any talk."

"Ramona, life is short. It's a beautiful summer night. Let's pick some of those magnolia blossoms over there"—

"Don't start," she said.

Taylor let her out at her apartment building, still half-expecting never to see her again. For a couple of days, he thought about their interaction, considered his own brooding, analytical manner, and decided that she wasn't looking for anything serious.

A few days later Taylor came home from an afternoon session at Tunica to a message from the Reverend on his answering machine: "Help. I'm back and stuck in this dump with Stormy and nothing to do. She's driving me crazy. Right now she's gone to get a manicure. May God be praised, she's out of here for a minute. You've got to take us to Tunica. By the way, I'm tapped. And if you're wondering why we need you to take us, it's because MGM Grand got my car. She bought us a bus ticket back. She won four or five hundred on the crap table—oh, I didn't get near the crap game—not that it made any difference. I repeat: the word is *help*."

Taylor had just returned from a losing session that afternoon—he had more or less stopped playing at Ramona's table because the personal connection between them was distracting—and hadn't made a penny all week. The Reverend had lost his two thousand and expected him to entertain his floozy. He might have declined, but he was seething with the injustice of the afternoon's loss. He called the Reverend and said, "I'll be there in fifteen minutes."

When the Reverend pushed open the screen door that scraped along on one hinge, he had the worried, sheepish expression of a loser. Taylor hated to see that look on his face. The Reverend had never had that look even during the worst of times at the county jail, where Taylor had first seen him, shuffling along in prison-issued flip-flops. From the jail, they had been sent to the county prison farm, and were locked up together for about six months. Taylor had received a Dickensian sentence for the entirely minor crime of borrowing money on a credit card that didn't belong to him, while the Reverend had been falsely accused of absconding with some backwater Church's funds, and there was yet another false charge on the Reverend, something pertaining to an irate husband and a gun which the Reverend waved off as beneath explanation. "Women often become enamored with the collar itself . . . an occupational hazard."

They had made a chess board out of paper, and Taylor discovered that the Reverend had a mind for patterns and sequences. Soon enough, Taylor had a plan for both of them. He traded three packs of roll-up and the chess set for a deck of cards, and in the echoing din of slamming steel doors and the howls of moronic convicts, an atmosphere not unlike a casino's, he dealt to the Reverend every night. After a couple of months the Reverend could count as fast as Taylor could deal. When Taylor got out, he stayed in touch, sending the Reverend a little money for the commissary, and when the Reverend had done nearly all of his eleven months and twenty nine days Taylor was waiting for him.

Now, for just a moment, Taylor regretted getting him into this. But it wasn't, after all, like the Reverend was going to seek honest employment. "Tough on the coast, huh?" Taylor said.

"It's tougher here," the Reverend answered in a low voice. "At least I could get away from her down there, what with me playing blackjack and her on the crap table. In this apartment, she's in my face all the time, and her return ticket isn't for two weeks."

Taylor glanced around, looking for signs of the girl. The Reverend had a couple of rooms and a kitchen, furnished with yard sale items and a torn flannel couch he had picked up from the sidewalk. The most expensive thing he owned, a snub-nosed .38, lay gathering blackness into itself on a cardboard file he used as a side table. A moribund picture of Jesus torn from a religious pamphlet was taped on the wall. Looking down, Taylor saw a tiny pair of golden high heels.

"Where is she?" Taylor asked.

"She's in the bathroom. She's been in there getting dressed since she got back from the manicurist, and don't expect her out any time soon."

"What's so bad about her?"

The Reverend leaned close, his eyes glittering, and whispered: "She's trailer trash. Has the mind of a harlot."

Taylor wasn't going to wait around for her, harlot or not. "Hey, Stormy," he called. "This is Taylor. C'mon out of there now, let's go. The tables are cooling off."

"Yeah, yeah," an unruffled voice answered.

Taylor and the Reverend sat down on the sofa and waited. Taylor could feel him fuming, as palpable an emanation as might have come from him if he had busted a dozen hands in a row. Where was the peace that passeth understanding which the Reverend advocated in prison last year while hearing confessions in a toilet stall, his services payable in honeybuns? Taylor was curious to see what she looked like, this woman he wanted away from so badly.

Stormy, who appeared to be about twenty-five years old, walked out of the bathroom. Words are sequential, and cannot convey her instant effect. Black pumps. Thin ankles. Tanned legs that looked as if she were wearing hose. A snug yellow sundress falling to the middle of her thighs, low cut and tight, hugging breasts about as big as nature makes them on a woman who isn't fat. Loose blond curls around her bare shoulders. A slight overbite, a pout, big blue eyes. She looked like a thousand dollar call girl. A little trashy, to be sure, but hell, Taylor liked trashy women. She was throwing herself at the Reverend, and he was complaining.

"If the tables are cold, I'll just warm them right back up," she said, holding her hand out to Taylor. He took it and felt something pass from her to him, something affirmative, like a promise. The Reverend tucked the thirty-eight into a shoulder holster beneath his denim shirt and the three of them walked outside, Taylor holding the door while the Reverend scowled. As they approached his old pickup truck, Taylor was sorry he was still driving it. He could have afforded something better, he told himself, but had been wanting to keep his stake liquid. The truck didn't even have air-conditioning. He opened the passenger side for Stormy. She put her hand on the seat and stopped short. "It's too hot in there," she said. "I'll sweat."

The Reverend snorted and rolled his eyes.

"No problem," Taylor said, peeling off his shirt and laying it on the seat. "You can sit on this." A gentleman's gesture, to be sure.

"Whatever," she said dubiously. Soon enough they were riding down Highway 61 with the windows open in a rattling, dented pickup, Taylor shirtless, the man of God on the other side with a demented gleam in his eye and a cigar in his mouth, the two of them looking like low-rolling rednecks. The only thing wrong with the picture, Taylor thought, was that the best-looking girl in the delta was sitting between them.

Taylor turned right at Lake Cormorant. "Most people think the road we just turned off is the famous highway," Taylor said. "But it's not. That's new 61." He drove down Starlanding Road for a while, bumped across some railroad tracks, and turned. Soon there were abandoned, rusting box cars on the left, looking primordial and menacing in the relentless sun, and on the right parched yellow fields with heat waves rising from them. Over there, out of sight behind the levees, the Mississippi River rolled, unaware that it had left its romance somewhere else. Taylor dodged the ruts in the road and said, "This is the real Highway 61."

"What's so famous about it?" Stormy asked.

He explained the connection with early blues musicians while she stared straight ahead resentfully. The Reverend, obviously, had been making her feel stupid. In profile, her pouting lips were more pronounced. Taylor wanted to put his arm around her.

They drove through billowing dust, passing gravel trucks while Taylor tried to stay off the shoulder of the narrow road—the deaths on this road would rise to battle levels before the state of Mississippi, in conjunction with the casinos, got around to finishing a four-lane highway—and soon enough the casinos appeared incongruously on the landscape, actually not unlike Las Vegas rising out of the desert . . . maybe more like Stormy sitting in his truck.

Inside Southern Belle casino, a spacious place with a relatively subdued notion of a Tara theme, considering the general over-the-top ambience of a typical casino, and a particularly nice blackjack pit, Taylor slipped the Reverend five hundred behind Stormy's back. These men of God have their pride. The air was cool, permeated with the distant dinging of slot machines and the indefinable smell of a casino: perfume and cigarette smoke, oiled wood and rank humanity, the scent of fear and risk. Ramona was pitching cards to a lone Asian woman whom Taylor had played with before, a competent player. Taylor scanned the pit quickly and saw that Ramona's table was the only one with the first and last positions open, which was where he and the Reverend needed to sit. As he led the way, the Reverend said, "Wait a minute. We're not going to play against Repo Ramona, are we?"

"C'mon," Taylor said. "First and third base are open. And she's not so bad. Her cards or her. In fact, Reverend, I've taken her out a couple of times while you were out of town." The Reverend squinted and said, "So, does that mean she's on our side or not?" They sat down, with the Reverend shaking his head. Ramona looked at Taylor and nodded slightly. Dealers are not allowed to deal to anyone the pit bosses know they have a connection with. She smacked her gum and said, "Gluttons for punishment, huh?" She wore her "been there—done that" tough broad attitude like a mask.

"We'll see about that," Taylor answered, smiling.

They sat out until the shuffle and then bought in at a hundred apiece. There was never any point in showing more money than necessary. A large buy-in drew immediate attention from the floor. A few desultory ten dollar hands went back and forth as the count climbed, coming into a favorable situation.

The woman in the center tapped out and got up, knocking her chair over in the process. She glared at Ramona and said, "You're cheating. I know you're cheating, bitch." Ramona stared at her levelly, just a hint of disdain playing around her mouth. The floor supervisor, who had heard the remark, came over and stood alongside the table. He looked at the woman quizzically and asked, "Ma'am, is there anything we can do for you?" Tears sprang into the woman's eyes as she turned and walked away. Taylor watched her go, more than a little surprised. He had seen her take a beating a couple of weeks ago with no more reaction than cold acceptance.

"You must have raked her across the coals," Taylor said. Repo Ramona shrugged.

Now it was the Reverend and Taylor. Stormy stood silently behind the Reverend, just watching. They both bet fifty dollars. Taylor drew twenty, the Reverend got a ten deuce; they were looking at a seven up. With the count being what it was, Ramona was almost certain to stand on seventeen, and the Reverend's only chance to win was to hit. However, because there was reason to believe that the next card was a ten, he stood, taking the loss but pushing that ten to Taylor on the next hand. Ramona turned over seventeen, shook her head at the Reverend's paltry twelve, and looked at him like he was something she had picked out of her teeth.

Stormy put her manicured hand on the Reverend's shoulder. Taylor couldn't help but be aware of her, steal glances her way while trying to keep up with the count, feel his heart swell with the thought of holding her tight on a spring morning with gauze curtains blowing in the flower-scented breeze, think this sort of thought while hoping that Ramona didn't see it scrolling across his forehead, and so on. She was a major distraction. "Do you want to play?" he asked. Luckily, she knew that they would do better on their own. "I don't want to break up the cards," she said. "I'm going over to the crap table." Ramona watched Stormy walk away, then met Taylor's eyes with a cold ironic gaze.

Taylor got up a couple of hundred out of the first shoe. "I hope you know that makes us even from the last time I played with you," he said to Ramona. "I don't think so," she said, smirking. "You cashed in five hundred on that session." Taylor was a little astonished. She was either paying particular attention to his wins and losses or had an incredible memory.

Taylor glanced away and saw Stormy over at the crap table. She was the shooter and had already gathered a crowd of men around her. A card bounced against his hand hard enough to give it a paper cut. At least it was an ace, since Ramona was going to make him bleed for it.

She started dumping, busting on every other hand. After thirty minutes, Taylor was up fifteen hundred and the Reverend had about seven hundred. Now, there is math, and there is intuition. Taylor knew that to play intuition was to lose. Still, there is a kind of indefinable card sense. A counter can beat the game of blackjack, but he cannot kill it. They had been killing it, winning too much too fast for the size of their bets. Taylor felt the cards getting ready to turn. He caught a nine and a deuce, looked at Ramona's five up, heard the blackjack god chuckle, and did not double his bet. Both he and the Reverend had a hundred out. Taylor scratched for a hit, looked at an ace, and stood at twelve.

The Reverend caught four eights and split them all, doubling on three of the hands. He played it by the book, to be sure, but the cards had not read the book. Taylor could feel him being reeled in. The Reverend just couldn't tell when he was being set up, couldn't tell because he wanted to win so badly. Taylor thought of the way the deck in Ramona's hand might have looked if they had turned it over and spread it before she began dealing. The Reverend would have seen the quadruple split waiting for him, like fate, whether good or bad remained to be seen, but Taylor had a sinking feeling. The Reverend had seven hundred dollars out.

Ramona hit four times, had three chances to bust, and the Reverend was screaming, "Come on with it, c'mon, bust!" by the end. Taylor felt the blackjack god's whip whirling over his head as she reached for the last card. Then the whip came down with a crack, and Repo Ramona turned over the perfect card. There it was, somehow inevitable. "Twenty-one," she said without a trace of emotion. She turned the Reverend's cards over and raked in his bets. He hadn't even tied, or "pushed," on a single hand. "Bye bye, seven hundred," Taylor said. It was a phrase he used when he had a big loss of his own and was trying to appear casual.

The Reverend leaned back, his face flushed with anger, reached into his wallet and put five hundred dollar bills—all he had—into the betting circle. "Money plays," he said. Ramona looked at him.

"Deal, goddamnit," the Reverend said.

"Wait, Reverend," Taylor said. "Let's take a break."

He glared at Taylor and for a moment his fury at his luck seemed to spill over. For just a moment Taylor felt a twinge of fear as he looked into the Reverend's eyes. He saw something ugly, something that could reach into the shoulder holster beneath his baggy shirt and come out with the .38 he *always* carried, which he had just carried past the NO WEAPONS ALLOWED sign at the casino entrance. Taylor continued to be surprised that the casinos had no metal detectors, unobtrusive or otherwise; possibly it had something to do with the loads of quarters and other change people used to carry around before the machines, whatever their price per pull, began accepting only bills and paying with vouchers. Maybe it was simply that the casinos were willing to take the chance for their customers' convenience. In any case, nothing at all changed even after an older couple was shot to death in the elevator, yet, of one of the Tunica casinos. Taylor watched the look drain out of the Reverend's face. "Oh, all right," he said, pulling back his bet and standing up. Taylor relaxed about any possible violence, but decided he needed to emphasize his reservations about bringing a gun to a casino.

They nodded goodbye to Ramona, Taylor emulating the sort of ironic friendliness that players and dealers who know each other only from the tables develop, while the Reverend scowled and Ramona remained stone-faced.

Stormy was still the shooter and five or six men were standing around her. A fat high roller with a wad of five hundred dollar purple chips in his hand was the closest to her. "C'mon, California," he shouted. Stormy shook the dice and called out, "Eight the hard way, just like the ladies like it!" Everyone, including the dealers, cheered. Taylor noticed the high roller put a green twenty-five dollar chip on top of Stormy's red five-dollar chip. "You're not betting enough, little lady," he said.

Stormy rolled a three. The fat high roller nodded at the dice red-faced and said, "She can be made. She's on the dice, ain't she?" According to the Reverend, he backed up the odds on his and Stormy's bet, a move which left Taylor perplexed since he did not know how to play craps. On the next roll, Taylor watched Stormy rake in about sixty dollars, thank the high roller with a sparkling smile, then put out her five dollar bet. "Let's see if we can do it again," the high roller said, putting a black hundred dollar chip on top of hers. If she was for sale, he was going to make the top offer. She rolled eleven, and raked in two hundred and ten. For the first time Taylor noticed her stack: she had a dozen hundred dollar black chips and a line of green twenty-five dollar chips along the table.

The Reverend tapped Stormy on the shoulder and said, "We're comped for dinner. Let's go."

"Not yet," Stormy said. "This table is hot."

The dealers were cheer leading. "C'mon, little lady," they screamed. "She's hot, fellows, she's hot." Stormy rolled an eight and as they pushed the dice back to her Taylor noticed two of the dealers exchange a sly smile. She rolled a nine and he noticed the same exchange. Something didn't seem right—what were they up to?—and he moved over behind them to try to see what was going on. Stormy rolled a six and this time one of the dealers looked over his shoulder and said to Taylor, "Check this out." Christ, all they were doing was "shortsticking" her, leaving the dice so far out on the table that she had to bend over to pick them up and they could see her tits. One of them said, "That's a beautiful sight, isn't it," and the other replied, "I'll give you ten to one on that." Stormy hit her point and jumped up and down, clapping her hands together rapidly at chin level like a little girl while her heavy breasts bounced. The high roller couldn't keep his eyes off her.

Taylor saw the Reverend lean in and now Stormy nodded her head. She picked up her chips and moved away from the table, then walked back to the high roller. Taylor went over to them. "Thank you, sir," he heard her saying. "You gave me four hundred and twenty five to play with, and here it is." The high roller looked like he was about to tell her to keep it when he saw Taylor and the Reverend standing behind her. "Well, thank you, little lady," he said, smiling at her, then looking at them. "I'm glad you won something with it." Naturally, she didn't offer to give him her winnings. "I didn't want to be obligated to him," she said as they were walking away. She had just cleared twelve hundred and fifty while risking five dollar bets of her own. There was a little spark in Taylor's mind as to Stormy's system.

They had crab legs and prime rib on the house and decided to pack it in. It had been a good night. Taylor had fifteen hundred, Stormy twelve fifty, and the Reverend had broken even in spite of the big loss on the split. They rolled north on old 61 under a bright moon that silvered the cotton fields. Stormy sat between them while the Reverend rested his head against the window and moped, having said nothing for fifteen minutes after lamenting Repo Ramona's last card with "What are the odds?" and it seemed to Taylor that Stormy was leaning closer to him. "I can still feel the adrenaline rush from the crap table," she said. Taylor breathed in her spicy perfume and something deeper, the musky scent of a gambler's excitement.

He knew what she meant even though he didn't want to acknowledge it. He always tried to win and lose with the same lack of emotion, to be as dispassionate as a computer. When he was first learning to count he remembered screaming "Yes!" after a couple of big hands, then realizing he had forgotten the count. The same was true of fear and frustration. During big splits, when a lot was riding on a single hand, he had sometimes made the mistake of concentrating so much on those cards that he would forget about the *next* hand, which is where counting always points. He knew the Reverend would have been unable to tell him the count after his split earlier. And frustration would kill a man, would make him bet five hundred dollars when he didn't know the count. Taylor tried to keep a check on all of his emotions when he was playing, consciously stifling jubilation or despair. Emotion would make a man misread the cards.

The Reverend hunkered down in his seat with his back to them and began to snore. Stormy talked to Taylor about her family, Vegas and Palm Springs. In spite of the associations with both places, he realized that she came from a poor family. Her mother was a gambler who now lived with her fourth husband, a preacher (probably of the Reverend's self-elected sort) who did not allow Stormy in the house. Her father, the third husband, was an electrician who lived in a tract home in the desert outside of Palm Springs. It began to seem a little clearer why she had decided to stay two weeks with the Reverend, whom she hardly knew. She probably had nowhere else to go.

When Taylor dropped them off she touched his arm and thanked him.

His arm warmed beneath the squeeze of her small hand. He watched her and the Reverend walk up the drive until they were inside. Pulling away, he found himself shaking his head, thinking about the Reverend's attitude toward her. Taylor was in no hurry to arrive alone at his apartment, where he would stare at the walls, hear the clock tick, and think about things that were behind him, and so he took an aimless, meandering route, like a superstitious Haitian who never walks in a straight line for fear of ghosts in his path.

Suburban houses began to thin. Out of the city, he turned at a bend in the road past maple trees silvered in the moonlight and a farm house appeared in front of him, as if framed in his windshield. The house blazed with yellow light and through a front window he saw a family gathered around a table. There were the parents at either end, two or three children . . . he saw a young girl toss her hair and laugh, and this sight gave him a very dismal feeling indeed. Sarah was gone . . . Ramona, Stormy, Lillian on the net, they were all just distractions to keep him from thinking about the fact that he had no house blazing with yellow light, no children inside it, and probably never would.

He felt disconnected from everything and everyone. His parents had died when he was in his early twenties; his mother unexpectedly from a heart attack; his father drinking himself to death as soon as possible thereafter. Taylor's older brother had inherited the house and essentially told Taylor not to let the door hit him on his way out. Using the house as collateral, his brother borrowed money for a hardware store, which went under promptly when a Home Depot was built a block away. The house was lost. So Taylor, in about a year, went from having a seemingly stable home and family to being alone in the world with no place to hang his hat. Even today, almost twenty years later, he would sometimes find himself driving late at night and turning toward his old house, wanting to go home. But there was no home to go to, and he had never really made one for himself.

Even when he was married, his house was always a place he was leaving, sooner or later. Either he or Sarah had always had one foot out the door. They had just started talking about children when they split up, and now it seemed a bit late to try to build a family—unless he could get rich quick. It remained to be seen whether that was in the cards. But this loneliness . . . it might have helped to talk to someone, maybe someone religious.

About an hour later Taylor found his way home and heard his phone ringing as he closed the door behind him. It was, in fact, a man of the cloth. The conversation, though, evoked little spiritual solace. "Listen," the Reverend said, "I've got to go to work tomorrow. I found a job unloading trucks, and I'm gonna do it until I find a place to preach or come to the end of this losing streak."

His stint at professional blackjack had lasted as long as his trip to Vegas. It was just as well. He didn't have the self-control a player needed, the self-control or the intuition. Any reasonably intelligent person could learn to count, but a real player knew when he was being set up.

"Stormy doesn't want to hang around the house with nothing to do," he said. "Can you take her to the casino?"

Taylor could do that.

WELCOME TO STARGATE, THE BEST THING ON THE INTERNET

Connect TRob Faulk

CONNECT

TRob says=My moles, all my moles . . .

Muffy says=Moles?

TRob says=So you're here today, little love. Are you not . . . my mole?

Muffy says=Not unless I'm sitting on your face.

TRob says=Well . . . are you?

Muffy says=Not today.

TRob: howls with utter abandon, the cry echoing down the empty streets of skid row, riding with a sheet of newspaper caught in the fetid wind, rising, falling, skidding across the pavement like a clumsy, dying bird.

Muffy says=OK, OK, for God's sake, I'm not in the mood for this. I'm your mole.

TRob says=Excellent. I'm feeling frisky today. Either frisky or anxious. I've got this nervous energy that needs to be released. Do you want to rob the bank?

Muffy says=You're going to get us in trouble, maybe even toaded.

TRob says=For robbing the bank?

Muffy says=No, but for the nasty things you'll probably say while we're doing it. Remember, no foul language.

Trob says=I will be a perfect gentleman. Besides, getting toaded's no big deal. Stargazer toaded me a couple of weeks ago. I was back on the next day under an assumed name.

STARGAZER INTERRUPTS: Little man, little man, I know everything that is said or done in our world.

TRob says=Madame Stargazer, please accept my humblest apology for my arrogance.

STARGAZER SAYS: Just remember that I see everything, TRob. Like cameras at a casino.

Soothsayer teleports in.

Soothsayer: looks at TRob with a mischievous grin.

Soothsayer: sways slowly toward TRob.

TRob says=Well, hello, ma'am . . . have we met?

Soothsayer says=We're just about to . . .

Soothsayer: puts her arms around TRob's neck.

TRob says=Ma'am . . . who are you?

Soothsayer says=Do you like me?

Muffy says=What's going on here?

TRob says=I like you very much . . . but, ahem, why have you conceived this instant passion? Or has my reputation preceded me?

Soothsayer says=I've got to see a person with my own eyes in RL before I believe anything.

Muffy says=What kind of slut is this?

TRob says=And do you have a naked GIF for me?—a picture on the internet?

Soothsayer says=Yes, I have one I call "The Wall," because it's me against a wall, being probed. But I accidentally deleted it from my files.

Muffy says=MUFFY YAKS!

TRob says=Curse our luck! But perhaps you can tell me what you look like.

Soothsayer says=Click on my description.

Soothsayer is a heavy-breasted blue-eyed blond in her late teens or early twenties, an impossibly beautiful girl that one sees on billboards. She has a tattoo that you haven't seen yet. Her personality is best described as passionate; her talent is the gift of prophesy.

TRob says=Maybe we could meet at a relatively private booth at the soda fountain. Or perhaps arrange a picnic down by the river. What are you doing at the moment?

Soothsayer says=Well, I'm at home alone painting my toenails. Do you prefer passionate red or innocent pink?

TRob says=Varied. Every other one. Say, are you, oh, none too bright?

Soothsayer says=None too bright? Well, I have lots of imagination . . .

some people think I'm maybe a little slow because it's so EASY to talk me into things . . .
TRob says=I think I'm smitten. Say, would you show me your tattoo?
Soothsayer says=Maybe later. It's in a private place.
Muffy says=If this doesn't stop I'm out of here.
TRob says=Soothsayer, maybe I could talk you into accompanying me to a hotel room?
Muffy teleports out.
Soothsayer says=Maybe . . .
TRob says=Let me go get one. Back to you in a flash, love . . . curious, huh, this sense of familiarity I have about you.
TRob teleports out.

Page Soothsayer=Room 227 at the hotel. Teleport in and we'll lock the door. Stargazer will know where we are but at least we're away from her prying eyes.
Soothsayer pages=I can't.
Page Soothsayer=Huh?
Soothsayer pages=I can't. The man I'm dating wouldn't like it.
Page Soothsayer=The man you're dating! Did he skip your mind when we met?
Soothsayer pages=No, he was exactly who I was thinking of.
Page Soothsayer=Well, that sort of escaped me . . . are you coming?
Soothsayer pages=Always . . . but not to the hotel room.
Page Soothsayer=C'mon, love. I will be a perfect gentleman. I find your name intriguing. I have some things I need to ask about, some things I need foretold.
Soothsayer pages=OK, but only to prophesy . . .
Page Soothsayer=By all means.
Soothsayer teleports out.

Taylor sat at Ramona's table, trying to block out any thoughts other than the cards. Ramona was extremely fast, but he had little trouble keeping up with the count if he didn't let anything distract him. Stormy came back from the crap table and hovered over his shoulder, looking morose. Obviously, she had tapped out. "C'mon, sit down," he said, getting up and giving her his seat at the full table. Ramona gave him a hard look. She didn't seem to care for his explanation that he was entertaining Stormy while the Reverend was occupied. "Just play that money there," he said to Stormy, pointing to about a hundred in chips on the table.

He stood behind her and watched her play low stakes. She was a decent player; she did not know basic strategy perfectly and did not know how to count. She was still better than ninety percent of the players in the casino. After a while the count went up and Taylor whispered to her, "Put twenty-five out there." When she was about to pick up her cards he decided to go out on a limb. Bending down, he whispered in her ear, "You're gonna get twenty." She picked up a queen and a jack. "I'm impressed," she said.

Stormy got on a run. She was raking it in and the count was still high, so when the novice next to her stood on sixteen against an ace, lost his last nickel and got up shaking his head at the dealer's outlandish luck, Taylor sat down in the empty chair and started playing again. It was Stormy's run, not his. After losing eight straight ten-dollar hands on busts, he couldn't stop himself from getting angry and pulling a hundred dollar bill out of his pocket. "Money plays," he said, trying to look confident.

The count had gone down and it was a fool play. A chance blackjack fell on Stormy's ten dollar bet, but once again Taylor caught a stiff. As he picked up his cards, saw sixteen, and glanced up at Repo Ramona to thank her kindly, she was already smirking at him. He busted; she snatched up Ben Franklin with a practiced gesture as he attempted to appear impassive. In fact, he was furious. That was nine hands in a row that he had busted while Stormy, right beside him, got twenties and blackjacks or hit to twenty-one on every hand.

He rubbed Stormy's shoulder. "For luck," he said, and put out two hundred and fifty. Stormy followed his lead, no doubt thinking that the count was high, and pushed fifty dollars into the betting circle. She got two kings. "Now I'm really impressed," she whispered. Taylor hit a twelve and busted. Ten in a row.

"Aren't you ashamed of yourself?" he said to Repo Ramona.

"Just the way the cards fall," she said, shrugging.

Incensed, he managed to resist the urge to put out five hundred, and pulled back to twenty-five, trying to look like he knew something. In point of fact, he had forgotten the count. Looking up, he noticed one of the pit bosses hovering around, the way they do when they suspect a counter and try to distract him. Stormy said softly, "I'm going to smile at him." She did, and said, "I like your suit."

"Thank you," he answered, hitching his lapels. "Giorgio Armani." Another floor supervisor appeared beside him, apparently interested in the cards. This second guy was young, a jiver from Philadelphia named Don with a line of gambler's patter. Taylor had made the mistake of getting friendly with him, and now he would come over too often when Taylor was playing and start talking, making him look away from the cards and lose track of the count. Taylor figured he would do that now, but Philly Don just stood over Stormy and stared at her. She looked up and said, "I like your cologne."

Taylor was waiting for Don's response when he noticed Repo Ramona turning over the player's cards. He had never seen anything like it. There were six players at the table—a double-deck pitch game—and on this hand every five in the two decks, all eight of them, had been dealt.

Additionally, every card was low; some of the players had hit three or four times. There wasn't a ten or an ace on the board. If there was ever a hand to bet on, it was the next one. He pushed five black chips into the circle and the table quieted down.

The bosses didn't notice. These two grown men were standing back from the table, playfully pushing each other, and saying, "She said she liked my suit."

"Yeah, well, she said I smelled better than you."

"Checks play," Repo Ramona called to get their attention, and they managed to look back to the game. The cards started going around. Taylor picked his up and looked at an ace/nine, ten or twenty. Repo Ramona showed a six up. Turning his cards over, Taylor pulled five hundred more from his wallet and doubled on the high count, expecting to get a ten and have the same hand with a thousand dollars out. "Gutsy move," Philly Don said. Taylor wondered if he was really thinking that it was a fool move. Maybe it was. The card was dealt down and he did not look at it.

Repo Ramona turned over a deuce, then hit with a three to eleven and Taylor's heart sank. Then she drew an ace. "There is a god," Stormy said softly. Now Repo Ramona was hitting from twelve, and everyone was expecting a picture. She hesitated. "Paint," Taylor screamed, unable to help himself. He watched her expression rather than the card and before it fell he knew it. With another dealer that gloating look of self-satisfaction might have been mock, might have meant a bust card. But not Repo Ramona. An eight fell. "Twenty," she said. All Taylor could reasonably hope for was a push.

She turned over the cards of the nickel betters first, taking all of them, and when she came to him she held her hand on the card for a second, looking at him with that hard, sardonic gaze. Taylor figured she was ready to rub it in about what a fool he was with his high-rolling bets and the pretty little floozy he was "entertaining." He felt his luck draining away.

The card just didn't look like a ten from the back. She turned it over and he didn't see color. Then he heard Stormy cheering before he could register the card through a swimming gaze. The ace of spades came into focus. He had hit a soft twenty with a one. He dropped his head on the table, unable to appear casual, and listened to Stormy's cheers.

Stormy's hand was on his back and he turned toward her, then hugged her to him, feeling her breasts give against his chest and watching out of the corner of his eye as Repo Ramona pushed out ten black chips. As he reached for the chips he thought he saw a little smile playing around the edges of his hard-hearted dealer's mouth . . . maybe she had gas.

They got up to cash in. As they walked toward the cage Stormy handed him all of her chips. "Here's your money," she said.

"Just keep what you won," Taylor said. "Come to think of it, keep the other hundred too."

As he heard what he was saying, the earlier spark about Stormy's "system" became a conflagration in his mind. This girl couldn't lose. She was a money machine. She gambled with other people's money.

The next week Ramona served him take-out Chinese reheated in a microwave. Taylor wondered if this was always her idea of "cooking." Her apartment was more spartan than Taylor had supposed, furnished simply but probably expensively with the kind of matching sofa and chairs one buys on time from a furniture store. The only thing that caught Taylor's eye was a computer on a desk in the living room. It didn't seem like the kind of thing Ramona would have at home.

"What do you do with that?" he asked, nodding at it.

"My husband left it here," she said. "He had to leave something."

After dinner they drove toward a movie theatre in his old pickup, which had become, much against his will, an embarrassment to him since he had registered how out of place both Ramona and Stormy looked in it. Like most people in the casino business, Ramona put a lot of emphasis on appearances; she drove a fancy Japanese sports car and always wore expensive clothes in a sort of preppie cast that was nearly the exact opposite of her demeanor—she was not above wearing tartan skirts and oxford cloth blouses. It seemed to Taylor that black boots and leather would have suited her better.

He considered how perplexing and difficult to place in any kind of context she continued to be. He was beginning to know the names of her favorite designers: Ann Taylor, Ralph Lauren, Liz Claiborne. His wife had bought her clothes at thrift stores but had managed to create, so her friends said, a "style of her own." The latter didn't keep up with his whereabouts because she was giving him "space to work on himself." He did have plenty of space in which to work, but it wasn't his wife who was on Ramona's mind: "This little blond bitch you're running around with . . . I thought you said she was your partner's girlfriend."

"She is. Like I told you, I've been having to entertain her while he works."

Taylor was beginning to realize that the only form of affection Ramona showed was jealousy. "I'll bet that's a chore," she said.

"Ramona, you don't need to worry about her. I'm not interested. She's way too young." Taylor hoped she didn't hear anything in his voice. Apparently she didn't, or at least decided to let it lie, and she lapsed into her silence, as quiet as something in a box. Taylor considered how little he knew about her.

"And what are your hopes and dreams, my love?" he asked.

"What do you mean?" she replied.

"I mean what do you hope for?"

"I was never like that. I never had time."

"Like what?"

"Like what you said."

"I don't follow you. I mean, what do you hope to get out of life."

Now she was getting irritated. "All I hope for is not to go out of my fucking mind. Is that good enough for you?"

They drove on in silence. What could be irritating about such a question? And could it really be true that she had no dreams at all?

"Ramona, I'm just trying to get to know you . . . I mean, I don't know anything about you. What your childhood was like, that kind of thing."

She fumed for a while, then jerked her head toward him: "You really want to know what my childhood was like?" She spit it out with the corners of her mouth turned down. "OK, what I did was *work*. I worked. My parents believed we should start early, so from the time I was eleven I cleaned houses after school and on the weekends." She glowered at Taylor resentfully, as if he had won something.

It was as if he had forced her to show one of her cards in a poker game, and it wasn't a good one. Not good to her, anyway. But whether or not it was good or bad depended on the other cards in her hand, the ones he couldn't see. He began to realize that she didn't know how to bluff, how to put spin on the facts of her life . . . she didn't know how to lie, it seemed.

"And now you're gonna want to know more," she went on, "so I'll just cut it short. You want to know what my life has been like? My life has been shit, and the only good thing that ever happened to me was my husband making me laugh."

Taylor felt his throat thicken. She was beginning to get to him. It wasn't so much that he believed what she said. It was the utter sadness that she believed it . . . and now he realized what her husband's leaving had meant to her. He pulled the car over, reached for her, and—without much abandon, to be sure—she fell into his arms.

They had driven far enough so that his apartment was closer than hers. Later, as they lay together on the futon, and Taylor tried to convince himself that his first time with anyone other than his wife in over ten years had been at least partially successful, he was aware that Ramona was not touching him, was simply lying behind him. She had a curiously missing affect. She was simply *there,* and Taylor kept trying to establish an emotional position, as it were, for the two of them so he would know how he looked to her as he lay on his side, desperately trying to sleep. He couldn't help but think of the comfortable feeling he would have had with his wife, how he would have known exactly what she was thinking. He rolled over and faced her. "Ramona, who are you? I don't know you."

"I'm the person lying here. The one you just screwed."

Something about the way she said the word didn't sound entirely sexual, and Taylor felt a kind of misgiving. He made an unsuccessful effort not to notice her cold stare, and would have given anything if her expression had softened, if she had said, "Just relax" or "I'm just enjoying myself being here"—even if she didn't mean it. The words would have been enough.

He turned back over and felt his stomach tighten. He wondered if she could hear him breathing, wondered if she was thinking about him at all. She seemed distant, unknowable, and it was their act of intimacy that made her seem so.

Two weeks passed . . . they lay together on the futon. He felt warmly enveloped in her limbs and familiar perfume. "When we move into the house," she said, "you'll have a workshop, we'll have dinners at home and take walks in the park, and you won't be living like this anymore."

Taylor let himself consider this scene of domestic bliss while looking at his water-stained ceiling with the missing plaster patches and feeling the gritty crumb-littered sheets beneath him. The prospect constituted an improvement, that was certain. "Of course," he said, "I have a couple of months to go on the lease here . . . I talked my landlord down to six months. He wanted me to sign for a year on this dump, for God's sake."

"There's no hurry. Just take some time for yourself to think about things. But remember, I have some expectations, and the most important one is that when we move back in together, there will be no gambling."

"No hurry for you, maybe, but your ceiling isn't raining down on your head," Taylor said, trying his best to hide his rising anger. Keeping his face carefully noncommittal as the sound of the word "expectations" resonated in his brain, he said, "No, no gambling." He tried to remember if there had ever been a time when he had been the one talking about *his* expectations. A flash of anger pulsed in his veins and he turned away, thinking that, yes, one of those expectations had been that a wife would not let her destitute husband go to prison because she wouldn't pay a credit card bill. What was she doing here anyway? This thing she had done . . . could she really have done it? And could he be expected to forgive it?

As to the matter of his duplicity, since he could not answer these questions, he had simply decided to play on until one of the women chose him or dumped him.

They saw each other two or three times a week, which was nearly as much as possible given her swing shift schedule at the casino. Ramona had not seen him with Stormy for a while so she had begun bringing up her other favorite topic.

"What's happening with your wife?"

"I don't know what's going to happen."

Her tone was cynical: "When you're ready to dump me and go back to her, let me know."

"That isn't going to happen," he said.

"What do you do at night when I'm at work and you're not playing?" she asked.

"I'm writing a story."

"What's it about?"

"It's about you, love."

"When you finish it, show me. I'd be curious to know how it turns out."

"You might not like it."

"That depends on who has the last word."

"Huh? I'm writing it. I suppose that would be me."

Ramona giggled. "You *think* you're writing it."

Taylor didn't care for the direction of this conversation, which seemed to be headed toward something new age or worse, so he didn't pursue it. He didn't want to hear about possession, or astral projection, or her special insight into who might be inhabiting his body incarnate at the moment. To the best of his knowledge at the time, nothing along this line was of any interest to Ramona, may God be praised. It never occurred to him that she meant something altogether different.

WELCOME TO STARGATE, THE BEST THING ON THE INTERNET

Connect TRob Faulk

CONNECT

Teleport to Soothsayer

PERMISSION DENIED

Page Soothsayer=Pardonnez-moi, m'lady Soothsayer, but in this dark and gloomy world, full of mendacity, obfuscation, crazed succubi and other, like, stuff, would you kindly consider responding in the affirmative to a poor tormented soul lost in the aforementioned Stygian darkness and his humble, beseeching request to observe the twin luminosities of your hooters?

Page Soothsayer=Soothsayer? Twin luminosities?

Page Soothsayer=SPEAK, STRUMPET!

Soothsayer pages=Uh, no.

Page Soothsayer=Come talk to me. I have Real Life problems.

Soothsayer pages=I'm busy.

Page Soothsayer=I've got to talk some more about this thing with my RL wife and girlfriend.

Soothsayer pages=So, you haven't worked that out yet?

Page Soothsayer=No, dear heart. No. I don't know what to do. I mean, I know how it will end with the girlfriend . . . I just don't know how to do it with the least possible hassle. You've got to advise me. . . . can I teleport to you? And by the way, why do I always have to find you on this game? Why don't we just trade e-mail addresses?

Soothsayer pages=No, of course not. Then you would know who I am.

Page Soothsayer=Oh, I think I have a pretty good idea.

Soothsayer pages=But you aren't sure, and that's how I want it. A girl needs her mystique, you know. Also, the game is fun. You can always leave a message for me with Stargazer. That's just like e-mail.

Page Soothsayer= Whatever you say, love. So, tell me where you are and I'll teleport to you.

Soothsayer pages=No, I'm talking to my boyfriend. Just page if you must. So, how will it end? And why are you calling me dear heart?

Page Soothsayer=I am calling you dear heart because you are a beautiful, beautiful child, and I adore you, and I am lost, and why are you wasting time with this dork of a boyfriend when you could be talking to me, Me, ME?

Soothsayer pages=A dork, huh? Maybe. But you ARE a pompous ass.

Page Soothsayer=Yes, and God, is it fun. Whatever. Hey! Now "whatever" is a term that shows I speak your language, sweet. Sort of like "stuff," which I trust you'll understand was included in my humble request in your honor.

Soothsayer pages=Go jump in a lake. And one more humble request and you're history.

Page Soothsayer=Go jump in a lake, yet. I won't bother at the moment with the limitations of your mode of expression. Let's be serious. I have a major RL problem and I need your help.

Soothsayer pages=How could someone like me with such a limited means of expression help you—a jerk like you, that is?

Page Soothsayer=You could help me because I love, need, and respect you.

Soothsayer pages=Love? Respect? I kind of missed that. You don't know the meaning of the words. What's more, you don't know me.

Page Soothsayer=Don't know you! What about the time I took you hostage (not so long ago, my love) and you were "somewhat willing"? And you will recall how you suffered the Stockholme Syndrome with me, and how the handcuffs excited you, and how . . . dare I say it . . . you *loved* me afterwards.

Soothsayer pages=Yeah, right . . . yawn. What have you decided about how your ridiculous RL affair will end?

Page Soothsayer=And furthermore, nobody really knows anybody anymore. You don't know where they're from, you don't know anything about their families, you don't know anything about how they were brought up because everything's ironic, and you can't tell whether their values are straight up or a send up. I could go on.

Soothsayer pages=Your ridiculous RL affair?
Page Soothsayer=I'm not sure, but I'm leaning in the direction you foretold, prophetess, so tell me how to dump my GF without making her mad. She might be—oh, how to express it subtly?—a psychobitch from hell. Not that I'm going back to my wife. There's, ahem, someone else in the wings. Say, would you like me to put my humble request in terms you can understand?
Page Soothsayer=Respondez-vous.
Page Soothsayer=SPEAK, STRUMPET!
THAT PLAYER IS IGNORING YOU.
Page Soothsayer=Please, please, please don't IGNORE me.
THAT PLAYER IS IGNORING YOU.
Page Soothsayer=PLEASE!
THAT PLAYER IS IGNORING YOU.
@ dis
TROB DISCONNECTS.

The Reverend called from work. Taylor caught the hollow sound of a warehouse telephone, then his voice: "I can't get off tomorrow, and she doesn't want to hang around the apartment with nothing to do. Can you pick her up and take her to the pool?"

"Yeah, that'd be okay."

Taylor's aunt had a large house with a swimming pool in the older section of Memphis. The plan had been for the three of them to take a break from playing and spend the day by the pool. Now it was just Taylor and Stormy.

The moment she got into the truck she started talking: "You ever do something and then you're sorry you did it?" she asked.

"Of course. What did you do?"

"It."

In response to his blank look, she repeated, "You know, *it*. I guess it's weird for me to be talking to his friend like this."

"What's the matter? Are you two fighting?"

"Not really fighting, no. He just doesn't like me. I mean, he doesn't come right out and say it, you know, but I can tell. He complains about the face I make when we play cards. When I wake up in the morning he's got his back to me."

"What face do you make?"

She wrinkled her forehead and held her tongue out of the side of her mouth and Taylor laughed. "All I can say is that if he's not in love with you he's out of his mind."

She was quiet for a moment as he drove. He breathed in her perfume along with the mown grass of the yards they passed. Taylor was reflecting peacefully that it was a beautiful morning when Stormy seemed to kick herself into gear. Now she was talking breathlessly, telling a story of how her mother had thrown her out of the house once when she stayed at Caesar's playing craps for three days without bothering to call and she had "winded" up staying with a woman who turned out to be a lesbian satanist and that woman and her husband tried to keep her locked in the house—"they wanted me for a love prisoner"—and how she had escaped and run into a man on the Vegas strip who took her home and they lived together and she danced in a topless bar while he gambled away her earnings. Then her mother let her come home, to a concrete block house set by itself in the desert.

Taylor wondered if her story was true, then thought that all stories, after all, were true in their way. They pulled onto his aunt's street. He suspected his aunt—of whom he had said nothing—and her house would be a little daunting for Stormy. A bit rich, a bit old south. His aunt was standing on the porch as he pulled into the circular driveway, a stern-looking woman in her seventies wearing a silk dressing robe and holding a silver cup. She looked formidable even to him. Stormy seemed to take it in stride, though. "By the way," Taylor said as he was parking the truck, "my aunt has old-fashioned morals when it comes to gambling. Don't mention it." Stormy nodded and smiled conspiratorially, then made the gesture of locking her lips and throwing away the key.

As they walked toward the porch, Taylor saw that his aunt was stone-faced and wished, equally, that he had prepared her just a bit more for Stormy. His aunt, after all, was close to his wife and was dead set against the impending divorce. Even though Taylor had made it clear that the girl he was bringing was merely a friend, someone else's out of town guest, his aunt obviously didn't like the looks of Stormy. But she was also incapable of being impolite. At the introduction, she said, "Stormy is a pretty name. Is it your real name or a nickname?"

"It's my real name," Stormy said. "My father named me after the 1970 Playmate of the Year."

His aunt struggled for countenance and Taylor said, "We can see why, honey. We can see why."

"There's a dressing room and towels at the end of the hall," his aunt said. Stormy smiled and walked away as the old lady watched her, then cut her eyes at Taylor.

"Like I told you," Taylor said, "she's a friend of a friend. A girlfriend of a friend."

"Uh huh," his aunt said.

Taylor was lying beside the pool in a lounge chair when Stormy emerged from the house in a silver bikini. From behind sunglasses he watched her walking toward the pool, diving in, climbing out on the other side, and for the first time he understood the origin of the phrase "gleaming limbs." He lay back, watching her. For a moment she seemed talismanic, heavy with meaning, like a sign of something that eluded him. What was she doing here? She dove in again, shook her head on surfacing, and gathered together the ghosts of his youth. Splashing up to the shallow end, she paused, looking pensive. "You know, I really liked the Reverend," she said.

Taylor thought he heard something strange about her accent, then thought about her use of the past tense. In point of fact, the Reverend hadn't seemed particularly likeable lately, not with his losing streak and his attitude toward Stormy. Taylor couldn't figure out what the situation was.

"You think maybe he's *trying* not to like me?" she asked. Before Taylor had a chance to think about it he replied honestly, "Why would he do that?" He saw Stormy wince just a bit.

"Maybe he's been hurt and wants to make sure it's right before he gets involved." Now he knew what he had heard. She had started pronouncing "like" as "lahk" and "right" as "raht." Taylor didn't talk that way, but it was her version of a southern accent. She was trying to fit in.

"Sometimes I think all men under forty are basket cases," she said. "Sometimes I think maybe I would do better with an older man, somebody I could learn something from."

Taylor leaned back in the sun and attempted to appear noncommittal. The Reverend was conspicuously in his early thirties while Taylor, on the other hand, fit the bill nicely. She splashed away and he lay watching her, letting his thoughts drift. He found himself wondering whether his wife had ever appealed to him the way Stormy did at this moment. Of course she had *appealed* to him, but in a very different way. As he thought of her, he couldn't help but smile: he had always liked her. Always, that is, up to the moment when he started gambling. At that point she had become a frightened and querulous grandmother.

He remembered the nights when he had gotten in a hole and played until dawn, and the screaming matches when he got home. And he remembered, very well, what she had said to him when she realized that he did not intend to quit: "When you get into trouble over this, don't come to me. I don't like it, and I'm not going to pay for it."

It didn't matter to her that he was winning. She wasn't a gambler. She didn't want to be married to one—and at the time that was fine with him . . . as long as he kept winning. He hadn't been interested in anything but the game for a long while anyway.

Then the big losses had come. At that point, he had not been a seasoned enough player to know just how badly the game could go. In disbelief, night after night he had watched the house take nearly every high count hand, hundred after hundred. He would sometimes arrive home without money for cigarettes and barely enough time to shower for his classes while Sarah screamed that this must stop, and all the time his assets were dwindling. Then he was playing on credit, running up cash advances, applying for more credit, trying to buy time until the cards turned and this aberrance abated.

One day a credit card came to the house in someone else's name, someone with his exact address but a different street: 3081 *Harbert* rather than 3081 *Harbor*. Taylor put the card in a drawer. The mailman, having made the mistake the first time, was apparently incapable of seeing it differently, and a couple of days later delivered the secret code. Taylor wrote the number on the card and put it in his wallet. This was something for only the most serious emergency.

That night was not long in coming. In a cold fury, he had played head to head with the dealer through a six deck shoe and had never won a single hand, pushing only two. How was this possible? Later, when he had read and knew more, he would understand that, given enough numbers, anything was possible, and that he had simply played long enough to see a manifestation of that possibility.

In the number pi, thousands and thousands of digits out, there are eight threes in a row. Taylor imagined a gambling game in which randomly generated numbers between one and ten are chosen. All of the numbers but three win. The minimum bet is fifty thousand dollars. *Someone* decides to play immediately before the first three, and this person never sees a win before he has lost his life savings, his house, his wife, his car, his clothes. He has made intelligent bets, bets absurdly more in his favor than he will ever encounter in any plausible gambling game, and he has lost 400,000 dollars. This person is, simply, unlucky. If he keeps playing, just one more hand, he will win, but he cannot keep playing because he is broke.

On the night of that implausible shoe, it had seemed to Taylor either that the house was cheating—an extremely difficult thing to do out of a six-deck shoe, although not impossible—or that he had been singled out by whatever forces as the unluckiest man alive. He grimly placed his last bets, the last money in the world he could borrow, onto two betting circles. He was dealt two twenties on the high count. The dealer hit to twenty-one. That was it. It was over. In three weeks, he had lost everything he had, including his good credit.

He got up from the table with his head spinning and at that moment remembered the credit card in his pocket. He marched to the ATM machine and withdrew five hundred dollars of a stranger's money. This, like everything in a casino, was recorded on videotape. The fact that Taylor knew this perfectly well was blanked out by his anger.

A month later, when one Mrs. Frederick Addison got a bill for a card she had never received, she called the bank that issued the card. The bank located the transaction, called the casino in question and asked them to look in the video files for a withdrawal occurring at 3:11 a.m. on February 4. One of the surveillance officers located the film and watched Taylor walk away with the money toward the blackjack pit. He then called in the floor supervisor who had been working that night and showed him the tape. "This guy here was playing at one of your tables a month ago. Do you know him?" The floor supervisor had no problem with that: "That's Taylor Robinson. He plays every day. You need his address?" The next day the police came to Taylor's home.

He was arrested and taken to the county jail. There, in disbelief, he heard Sarah say over the telephone that she would not post his bail. What about his job? That was his problem. Looking back, it was strange to think that he had never even called the college where he had worked for ten years to explain his absence, but what was there to say? He supposed Sarah had told them where he was. From the jail, he went to the county penal farm for six months, and when he got out, he went back to his home with her because he had nowhere else to go. He had planned to live with her until another option presented itself. For that, he needed money. And there was one last asset. It took a couple of weeks for him to withdraw his retirement fund and then he began playing again.

That was when Sarah left. He understood completely, given her perspective. It didn't matter to her that the bad spell was over, and that he was winning again. Maybe he wouldn't have wanted to be married to a gambler either. But when he had accepted her leaving with such apparent ease, he had not known then that staring down at a table and the cards that fell before him would be so lonely when there was no one waiting at home.

Blackjack is a cutthroat game. In spite of the fact that the counter supposedly *knows* he will win in the long run, Taylor was never sure. Still, he loved the game because it was pure. If a novice won and he lost on a given day, the novice was the better player on that day, because the bottom line told it all. The blackjack god, though, would get it back from the novice. Taylor intended to keep his. Lately, though, he had been courting trouble again, betting too high, losing too much. If his edge from counting didn't assert itself soon, he could lose his retirement money too. All of it. He could be delivering pizzas at the age of forty-two while his wife and former friends kicked up their heels, not only in celebration of their own good sense, he thought, but at the justice of the payback for his philandering karma.

Taylor watched Stormy bounce high off the diving board, form a silhouette against the sun, then leave a silver streak on the surface as she disappeared into the blue. A loser didn't win a woman like her . . . part of him continued to watch her, another part leaned back in the sun and ran through a deck of cards.

He pursued his thoughts as he lay there by the pool, dipping in occasionally, drinking cold beers that his aunt was kind enough to bring out on a Chinese tray. It was a spectacularly hot July Memphis day, and at some point he noticed he was lightheaded. Stormy came and stood over him, shaking herself. She smelled like sunshine and coconut oil. Cool drops fell from her breasts to the bright sun on his chest. "Come back in," she said. "It's wonderful."

They dove together into the cool blueness and Taylor had a kind of vision, whether from the heat or what he did not know. Huge cards shimmered. For some reason Ramona's hands appeared vividly, swaying with that curious flick of her wrist as she dealt. Stormy swam underwater through a sparkling blackjack, her feet flashed, and then she was out of sight. The crude embodiment of the cards fell away and numbers floated, shifted, rearranged themselves, then the numerals themselves fell away and he was in a world of abstract, invisible values. He could sense them shifting around him, and for just a moment he thought he sensed a pattern in the chaos. Then it was gone, and it was as if he was looking at the back of a card, the dealer's down card, and he couldn't tell what it was.

He surfaced and looked around him. In that moment, the world no longer seemed like a watch whose workings could be understood once the facts were revealed. There was more to it, something in the darkness on the other side of things. Stormy came up beside him and hung on the edge.

"Why are you looking at me like that?" she said.

"You're a little bit of magic, you know?" he replied.

She smiled a model's smile, then pushed herself to arm's length and arched her back, thinking he was talking about her breasts.

Taylor was lying on his futon taking stock of his bedroom and fighting off an unsettling mood when his eye came across a bookshelf he had placed in the one spot in the apartment where it would fit. He was still attempting to put his belongings back together from the various storage places and friends' garages where they had landed. Suddenly the bookshelf came into focus, numinous and foreboding. Something shifted in the back of his brain. He reached for the phone and called Sarah.

She answered in her welcoming way. Her voice had the tone of someone proceeding with her life, not wallowing in a divorce. "Sarah," he said, "this bookshelf, the tall one I have. Where did we get it?"

"Don't you remember?" she asked.

"I'm not sure," he said.

"Of course you are. We bought it at a yard sale seven or eight years ago at the same apartment you're living in."

Taylor's heart skipped. Suddenly he remembered the young couple sitting on the front steps: a shirtless man in his twenties, wearing jeans, a pretty girl with unbrushed hair for whom he felt an instant affinity. He remembered her eyes meeting his and holding, and she had seemed slightly sad, a bit down and out. He remembered the front door of the apartment standing open, the pieces of newspaper scattered across the floor.

"So you're telling me it came from here?"

"Yes."

"There's only one wall here that it fits against. It has to be in the same place that it was. Don't you think that's strange?"

"Quite a coincidence," she said, a little nonplussed. After all, these things happen.

He said goodbye and lay staring at the bookcase as if it were forensic evidence. He tried to remember what he had been thinking that day as he had glanced into the open door of the apartment. Had there been anything telling him that this place would mean something to him? He could remember a sense of empathy with the couple, a sense that they might have been him years before. Now it was years later and he was looking at their bookshelf in the same place where they would have seen it. In a sense, he was looking through their eyes, and the bookshelf had made its way back to where it apparently was meant to be. Again he thought of the girl with the unbrushed hair and the moment their eyes met. It *had* been as if she were trying to connect, to reveal something to him. A chill went up his spine.

The phone rang and he reached for it instantly, thinking it was Sarah. But it was the Reverend, who said, "Listen, can you take her to the casino a couple of times this week? I'm gonna be working."

"Sure," he said. "I'm going tomorrow afternoon."

In the morning he spoke for an hour to the psychologist with whom he had had sporadic appointments since his separation—not about his impending divorce, not about gambling—the psychologist's favorite topic—not about Stormy, but about Ramona. His wife was becoming more and more distant as it became apparent that he was doing *something* with his time, and she probably knew perfectly well he was still playing, although she was perhaps yet unaware of the girlfriend. Since gambling was basically an impasse with the psychologist—Taylor had no intention of stopping—to bring up the subject of his wife would bring up the psychologist's favorite, so Taylor didn't. Stormy was a phenomenon, an ephemera, he suspected, as unreachable as a shooting star. Ramona, on the other hand, was becoming part of his life. There would come a time, he imagined, when she would open herself to him.

He was of the opinion that, as her defensiveness manifested itself, she would set herself up to be taken advantage of, as it were, and would unconsciously attempt to create the very thing she feared. Together, he and the psychologist considered the angles, the nooks and crannies, the picture from its various perspectives. And as they did this, he was formulating what he would say to Ramona. After the session he thought about it for a couple of hours, and made some notes. One thing he knew for sure: her interior life was dark. There was a haunted quality about her, and it was haunting him.

The next time they saw each other he pulled the car over on the way to the theatre. About half the time they never got to the movies they had intended to see.

"Ramona," he said, "I want to talk to you."

"Uh oh," she said.

"I've thought a lot about this, and I just want to say a few things. You know, I spoke with my therapist about you."

"I thought you were supposed to talk to a therapist about yourself."

"Well, talking about you is talking about me, I mean, I was talking about us . . . our *relationship.*" The word hung heavy in the air. He half expected her to say "What relationship?" but she said nothing.

Taylor began speaking carefully, attempting to sound spontaneous with words which he had nearly memorized: "Now, for whatever reason, you're extremely defensive. You have your guard up, as you say. In order to get past this guard, well, it requires a little courting, my love. It's the nature of the situation. The catch is that the more you care about me the more your guard will come up. To care for someone is to be vulnerable. And that's what you fear more than anything. You don't want to be out there with big money. But Ramona, love is a gamble." He particularly liked this last metaphor, which he had carefully chosen because she would find it familiar.

"Why do you talk about all this stupid shit?" she said.

Taylor sat back, a little stunned, trying to swallow anger.

"Look, what is it about me that you like?"

"I can have an orgasm with you."

The next day, as they walked in a park through a path of blossoming dogwoods and he tried to shake off the anxiety generated by lack of sleep, he asked her if he seemed "exotic" to her.

"Exotic? No."

That was it. No further explanation, no nod at all toward the connotations of the question. He felt foolish and halting as he tried to explain that she did seem that way to him, "exotic," as she stared straight ahead, poker-faced. The subject finally died when he stopped torturing it, and he looked around for another. "This is a beautiful day," he said, "with silver lacing around the edges of an azure sky."

"I hate the way you put things," she said. "And it's hot."

Well, it was a little hot.

"You wanna know how you seem to me?" she asked.

"Yes, of course I want to know."

"Married."

Stormy got in the truck and smiled. "I've got my lucky charm today," she said, bending toward him and showing him both cleavage and a necklace with a little pair of golden dice hanging from it. She was dressed like a parody of a southern country girl, like a kissing cousin, with a white blouse tied just below her breasts and a denim miniskirt, then black pumps.

After they had driven in the heat for a while, she reached into her purse and pulled out an atomizer. Curling her legs up on the seat, she sprayed them, then turned the atomizer on her neck and bare stomach. "What's that?" he asked.

"It's water. Keeps me from sweating. You want some?" She handed him the bottle and he looked around for some bare skin to spray it on. "I don't have any place to spray it."

"Here, silly," she said, taking it from his hand and spritzing his face. It felt cool and good. She started spraying her legs again and he noticed that she didn't shave them all the way to the top. Halfway up her thighs, light golden hairs played against her tan.

She told him a story about how she and her father used to go dancing and how an older man, an attorney, used to dance with her now and then. When the attorney had found out six months later that the man she had been dancing with all that time was her father, he had said, "I've been wanting to ask you out for six months. I thought he was your boyfriend."

"My father looks young, like you do," she said. "My rule of thumb is

I don't date anybody older than my father. He's forty seven. But I don't think somebody early or mid-forties is too old for me. Do you?"

"No, not at all," Taylor said. The count was rising.

At the casino Stormy sat for just a moment at the blackjack table, then went to play craps. Taylor was settling in at Ramona's table when Philly Don, the young pit boss, came over to him. "I don't mean to be nosy," he said, "but that blond lady—is she your wife?"

Ramona gazed at Taylor coldly and shuffled the cards with an ominous snap.

"No," he said. "She's just a friend."

"A friend, huh? Hard not to notice her. These southern girls, I don't understand them. They expect you to be a gentleman."

"She's from California," Taylor said coldly, and looked down at the sixteen he had just been dealt.

Philly Don hovered for a minute and then walked away.

Taylor got on a run and started betting more than he should have. No doubt he was hoping to impress Stormy with a big win. But he was having some luck. After a while Stormy pushed through the knot of people that had gathered behind him to watch the action. She sat down beside him and pushed a nickel into the betting circle. He rubbed her shoulder rapidly. She looked at his hand on her shoulder and said, "I'm peeling."

When he turned back to the table Repo Ramona was scowling at him. When she was like this, it brought out something competitive in Taylor and she became just a bitch dealer he was out to beat. He guessed she didn't like him rubbing Stormy. "She's my good luck charm," he said.

"That's a good thing to bring to a casino," she said, world-weary and tired, tired of gamblers.

Taylor pushed ten black chips into the betting circle, a thousand dollars. She dealt him an ace/seven, a soft eighteen, and she showed a six up. He was going to beat Repo Ramona again. He reached in his wallet and counted out ten one hundred dollar bills next to the black chips. "Double down," he said. As in the earlier double, he was expecting a ten, which would give him the same hand with more money out, but he got another miracle hit: a deuce, which gave him twenty.

Strangely, the kid on his other side, a rank novice who had sat down quivering with excitement like a bird dog on point, introduced himself with "I'm Jack. Gambling's my game," and whom Taylor had pointedly ignored, had exactly the same hand. He poked his finger at it and said, "Eighteen?" Ramona, automatically responding to the gesture calling for another card, started to hit it when Gambling Jack held his hand up. Taylor saw the card before she pulled it back. Christ, it was a four, which would in all likelihood give her a twenty also if the moron didn't take it. That card would keep Taylor from winning two thousand dollars. "I didn't want a hit," Jack said. "I was just asking what I had."

"Take the hit," Taylor said. Jack was betting a nickel. Taylor pushed him two red chips, making his hand a winner.

"I don't hit eighteen," he said.

In desperation, Taylor hissed, "It's a four," and then nodded toward Ramona's up card, the six. "She's gonna have twenty. Take the hit." Ramona remained stone-faced.

Third base had also seen the card, and apparently thinking that the game would proceed in spite of everyone's prior knowledge, bellowed, "Take the goddamn hit! The next card's a four." Philly Don, who had been standing near another table, heard him and walked over. "What's going on?" he asked.

"I don't hit eighteen," Jack said again, unable to understand the situation.

Philly Don looked at Ramona questioningly and she turned over the four. "I exposed this card," she said. Taylor saw Stormy give Don her most heart-breaking smile. Don was sharp, and it didn't take him a second to assess the situation. He looked at Stormy again—she had fifty out, a large bet for her—and made up his mind. "Sir, if you point to your cards you must take the hit," he said to Jack. "I'm sorry. Be careful with your hands next time." At that moment, as his heart swelled with gratitude toward Don, Taylor understood Stormy's inestimable value.

Ramona pushed the four to Gambling Jack, and then, before anybody had a chance to think about it, the idiot scratched for another hit, not satisfied with his twelve. Taylor watched the card fall on the table as if a pigeon the bird dog flushed had just flown over: a king—Ramona's bust card. Third base was standing with a thirteen that he had flashed to Taylor. Everyone, including Philly Don, looked at Jack in disbelief. He shrugged. He'd lost his nickel. He was oblivious to what he might have just done to the rest of them.

Repo Ramona turned over her down card. A ten, as it should have been. Now she had sixteen. With something akin to a shrug, she dealt herself a five. "Twenty one," she said coldly.

"Stand up, you ignorant bastard," Taylor said to Jack as he rose from his seat. Gambling Jack looked up, perplexed. The next thing Taylor knew strong arms closed around him from behind, and security was escorting him from the casino, with Stormy tagging along behind, calling out, "I'll be there. I've got to cash in."

In the car Taylor was silent and grim as they started for home. Somewhere along 61 Stormy put her hand on his shoulder and said, "The reason you're so mad is because you're not just playing for money, you're playing for pride." And the Reverend thought she was stupid. She was right, of course. She had a head start, anyway. "And Repo Ramona knows that you should have won that hand," she added. "It's okay. You'll win it back in the long run." Stormy, who could not be unaware that Taylor and Ramona knew each other, thought the relationship was competitive. He had not mentioned the personal aspect.

He glanced at her. She was looking straight ahead down Highway 61, sort of driving with him because the road frightened her. He thought of the bluesmen who had traveled this road, thought of Big Joe Williams traveling so fast at sixty he "could hardly hold the wheel." He thought of Stormy and himself flying toward freedom. She was prettier than six-seven-eight on a purple chip. Something turned over inside him.

"Stormy," he said, "Do you think the Reverend will come out to Vegas to see you?"

She was quiet for a moment and then said simply, "No, I don't think so."

"I'd like to come out there and play with the surrender option," he said. "I mean, I'd like to come out even if the Reverend doesn't come."

"I'd drive up from Palm Springs to meet you," she said.

Blackjack? He couldn't be sure.

"Tomorrow's her next-to-last day," the Reverend said on the telephone. "If you'll take her down there one more time I guess I can entertain her Saturday. Then, finally, she'll be out of here."

"I've got one question for you, Reverend. What is it about her you don't like?"

"C'mon, man. She's trash."

Taylor said goodbye and lay back in bed, staring at the ceiling. The thought came to him that his wife was probably not sleeping alone. He remembered the way she would throw a leg over his in her sleep. What did Stormy do in the night? He could almost feel her put her head on his chest, almost smell her scented curls. There was her small hand trailing across his stomach, the look in her blue eyes as he turned toward her. After awhile, he got out of bed and paced around the room, then sat down at the computer. Maybe Soothsayer would be there, in the virtual world.

WELCOME TO STARGATE, THE BEST THING ON THE INTERNET

Connect TRob Faulk

CONNECT

Teleport to Soothsayer

PERMISSION DENIED

Page Soothsayer=Tell me you would walk through fire for me.

Page Soothsayer=Respondez-vous.

Page Soothsayer=Tell me you would throw yourself between me and a rabid purple-assed baboon.

Page Soothsayer=Well?

Page Soothsayer=This is royal fun. Tell me you would piss on me if I was on fire.

Soothsayer pages=Yes, I would do that.

Page Soothsayer=Let me teleport to you, seeress. I am a poor soul tormented in Stygian darkness tonight, and I need help.

Soothsayer pages=Soothsayer rolls her eyes.

Muffy pages=Sorry to interrupt, ol' buddy. Long time no see.

Page Muffy=Well, I've been around. You just haven't been looking for me and I've been sort of hooked into Soothsayer.

Muffy teleports in.

Muffy says=You know, you don't know much about this Soothsayer.

And are you still trying to get that thing with your wife and girlfriend worked out?

TRob says=I know enough, and yeah, more or less, except maybe there's someone else in the soup now.

Muffy says=Someone else, yet. You're a live one, TRob. I'll get back to that, but for the moment let me stay on the subject. Don't you feel a little silly, Mr. Mid-Forties, trying to get advice from Soothsayer, an eighteen-year-old girl?

TRob says=Of course. It's absurd. But then, I always liked the absurd.

Muffy says=Well, you've got it. But not the way you think. You told me Soothsayer said she was from out west . . . don't you know how to look for the location of someone? She's in Memphis, just like you are.

TRob says=You can tell? Hmmm, I think I already knew that, love . . . but no matter. She's still a prophetess, as we know by her name.

Muffy says=There's more . . . it's absurd to be getting advice from an eighteen-year-old, but guess what? Soothsayer used to be on here under another name (according to one of her cybersex friends) and she wasn't eighteen then.

TRob says=I think I knew that too. The facts of her life are incidental, and subject to change. The factuality of her prophecies is what concerns me, good buddy (TRob pats you on the head). And now, hasta libido.

Muffy says=Wait! Muffy sits on the windowsill, leans too far back, says, "Help! I'm umop episdn!"

TRob says=Very cute, love. . . TRob pulls you right side up, shuts the window and says searchingly, probingly, firmly but gently, "Now I have RL problems to deal with. I will take my leave . . . and you stay away from that window.

Muffy says=OK, but don't look for RL answers in VR. . . a word to the wise.

Page Soothsayer=Where are you? Let me come.

Soothsayer pages=All right, you can come for a little while. Room 227 at the hotel. I'll unlock the door.
Teleport to Soothsayer
Soothsayer: Soothsayer is half-reclining on a day bed set on an oriental carpet in this room illuminated by candle light. She is surrounded by silk throw pillows. Sitar music plays in the background. The smell of ganja is almost obscured by the heavy incense in the air, a mixture of cloves and orchids. She is wearing a bright Indian sari loosely tied at the waist. One of her legs is bent slightly so the sari falls away from her thigh. Her brown hair billows across her piercing green eyes.
TRob says=Prophetess, you look strangely like my girlfriend tonight. You've changed your hair color.
Soothsayer says=Do you want me?
TRob says=Very much.
Soothsayer says=What a surprise. But I don't cheat on my boyfriend.
TRob says=Oh, c'mon. What he doesn't know won't hurt him.
Soothsayer says=I would know.
TRob says=So what? This is just a fantasy . . . just words.
Soothsayer: stretches on the pillows, and you notice that the rich brocade of the Byzantine designs on her sari depict sex acts. She pulls the tie so that it falls open and her breasts are revealed. She lies back on the pillows and looks into your eyes . . . TRob, does this look like a fantasy?
TRob says=Well, yes and no. But why did you change the color of your hair? Your eyes too, for that matter. Why do you look so much like her?
Soothsayer says=Guess.
TRob says=No time today for games. Tell me what I should do so that she doesn't get crazy when I put an end to things . . . I've begun to get an eerie feeling . . .
Soothsayer says=There is nothing you can do.
TRob says=But there must be a better course. A lesser evil. Tell me what

to say so that this psychobitch doesn't go off the deep end . . . hell hath no fury, as you know.

Soothsayer says=You've made your choice.

TRob says=Not exactly. I've decided to dump the succubus, yeah, but I don't think I'm going back to my wife. And maybe not to the young one I've been telling you about. Maybe I should look for someone else, someone my age, someone with whom I have something in common. Hmmm, what do you think?

Soothsayer says=Come here, hold me, and I will whisper it to you.

Soothsayer: parts the sari with her raised knees, reaches her arms out to TRob.

TRob: goes to Soothsayer, lies down beside her.

Soothsayer says=Gotta go! Bye bye.

SOOTHSAYER IS GONE.

Teleport to Soothsayer

PERMISSION DENIED

Page Soothsayer=You day-tripping two-timing prick-teasing floozy, TELL ME!

THAT PLAYER IS IGNORING YOU.

Page Soothsayer=TELL ME!

THAT PLAYER IS IGNORING YOU.

@ dis

THERE IS A MESSAGE FOR YOU FROM SOOTHSAYER

@ Retrieve message

I see hard luck coming for you, gambler.

@ dis

TROB DISCONNECTS

They walked in the park. Taylor took her by the arm and guided her toward a wisteria-covered gazebo. Feeling her arm give through the silk blouse almost did something to him. "Let's sit here on this bench," he said. She sat at her discreet distance, and he said, "Ramona, I want to show you something." He had found something which he considered a clear illustration.

"What?" she said, suspiciously.

He pulled out two magnets he had bought that morning at a hobby shop and put them down between them on the bench. "Watch. See, when I pull this one away, the other one follows. But if I turn it around where they are facing each other, the other backs away."

She watched while he felt something building up inside her. Then she looked up and said, "So fucking what?"

"This is what you're doing."

Her eyes flashed. "You don't know a goddamn thing about what I'm doing," she said.

"Don't you see you're creating the thing you're afraid of?" he asked.

She got up and started walking. He sat for a moment, then trotted after her. Life was short. It was a summer day. Such as it was.

The next night he was about even on the blackjack table and Stormy was up a couple of hundred from betting other people's money on the crap table when they broke for dinner. They were comped for Steamer's, the high roller restaurant at Southern Belle. They ate free steak and lobster and she told him tales of California. At one point she steered the conversation back to the Reverend. "I looked across the crap table at Caesar's and he was looking at me," she said. "I knew we would see each other again."

Why did she keep talking about the Reverend? She and Taylor obviously got along. They could travel together. He could beat the blackjack games and when he lost she could take up the slack. With a little run of luck they could build up a bankroll that would get them comped at the best places in Vegas. He thought of them lying in one of the king-sized beds at the honeymoon suite at Caesar's Palace, ordering from room service. He remembered having the best pastry of his life at Caesar's, and as it melted on his tongue and he closed his eyes, he had envisioned a man on the top floor in a room ringed with safes full of cash. This man was wearing a black shirt and, of course, a white tie, and said to an assistant, "Mario, go over to France and buy me a cook, and don't let him be a disappointment."

Stacking a dream on a dream, Stormy was saying, "Later that night at Caesar's, he took my hand and started talking like this." She took Taylor's hand in hers and began mumbling words which at first he couldn't hear above the beating of his heart, some sort of schlock from *Gone With the Wind*. He couldn't imagine the Reverend saying those sorts of things, nor could he imagine that this was happening now: Stormy looking into his eyes as he felt the heat of her soft hand, saying, "I loved you from the moment I saw you." She held onto his hand until he pulled it away. "And when I come here he acts like this," she said after a moment.

After dinner Taylor didn't feel like playing. "Let's head back," he said, wanting to be alone with her and realizing that this drive would be their last. He was silent for most of the time, and as they pulled into the city he realized that his only chance was dwindling away. He kept looking for a place to pull over and say those same kinds of things. Stormy had kept up a more or less steady stream of one-way conversation, and as he pulled onto the Reverend's street he heard her say, "I hope when the Reverend gets older he looks like you, because to me you're really good-looking."

Taylor whipped the truck to the curb. Just before he spoke he noticed she had a frightened look on her face which should have given him pause; however, like a man throwing good money after bad, he wanted this thing to be in the cards so much that he couldn't stop himself. "Stormy," he said, "can I kiss you?"

"No!" she said, actually looking surprised.

Bye bye, one thousand. "Okay," he said, shrugging. "It was just a thought."

He pulled the truck immediately back onto the street and started driving. Suddenly he felt sorry for her, this girl alone in a truck in a strange city getting hit on by a middle-aged man. After a moment she said, "That would really complicate things, don't you think?"

Taylor shrugged again, trying to salvage his dignity. "It was just a thought. But don't forget I had it."

She had given him all the signs. Maybe she needed time to realize it herself. They were silent. He let her out at the Reverend's house and watched him open the door. At that moment he was certain she would call tomorrow and tell him she hadn't forgotten. Then they would set things up for Vegas.

The next morning his phone rang early. He awoke instantly and grabbed the receiver. "What are you doing making a pass at Stormy?" the Reverend asked.

Taylor felt adrenaline surge in him like a shot. "Let me talk to her," he said.

"She's gone. I took her to the airport early."

Taylor took a deep breath but his voice still shook: "I would never have done that if I thought you were interested in her."

"Yeah, right, you bastard," he said. "It's a good thing I'm not. But she was sure trying to make me interested by telling me what you did. Trying to make me jealous—like I give a shit."

The Reverend hung up and Taylor propped himself on an elbow and stared at the crumbling wall until his heartbeat subsided. Then something came to him with crystal clarity.

Stormy had set him up.

There was only one thing to do to get his mind off the girl, Taylor thought. He pulled on the clothes he had worn the day before and, without bothering to call the Reverend, brush his teeth or run a comb through his hair, headed south. If he had known what was coming, he would have worn a tuxedo, or at least a white tie with a black shirt.

That afternoon he played recklessly against Repo Ramona, simply letting his wins ride half the time regardless of the count. The cards got stuck in one of those amazing runs that always happen when you're betting nickels, but this time Taylor asked Philly Don to raise the table maximum, which he did obligingly, probably figuring the house would get its money back that much faster. But the cards didn't change and the chips kept coming out of the rack, first green, then black, finally purple. "What the hell," Taylor thought. He didn't feel like protecting a win. "Let it ride," he kept saying.

It was the best run of cards he had ever been dealt and he wasn't getting any juice from it. He met Ramona's gaze. She was wearing her usual cold, cynical expression but beneath it there was something encouraging him, pushing him on. Take it down while your winning, man. Take it down. He placed another tall stack of black chips into the betting circle. Win or lose, he didn't care. The run went on. He kept pushing out huge bets, part of him daring the cards to confirm the way he felt. They would not do it. They kept falling like hope and magic in front of him.

At the shuffle he stretched and sensed something. Astonished, he turned around and saw a crowd of about fifty people gathered behind him. He looked back to his chips. Yes, it was a pile. Behind Ramona, five suits were staring at him coldly. He looked at her, and the encouragement was gone, replaced by something else entirely. Maybe she was right: maybe playing on would amount to being just another fool gambler.

"Color up," he said.

The process of exchanging smaller chips for larger ones took a while. The suits oversaw the procedure officiously and then Taylor was stuffing purple chips into every pocket while he heard muffled comments and gasps from the crowd behind him. He turned and walked through them to the cage, not meeting anyone's eyes, not feeling much of anything.

He cashed in and drove over to Sam's Town, the first casino in Tunica to have a hotel. He didn't want to go home alone. He rented a room and lay there by himself, staring at the ceiling. Things were maybe a little better now, but they weren't good. There was no order in his life, no center, nothing and no one to be faithful to. His wife was pulling away. Stormy had betrayed him. Ramona was cold. Maybe now, he thought, he could buy somebody to care about him. Over on top of the television, in a brown paper bag he had picked up off the casino floor to put the money in, lay fifty-seven thousand dollars in cash.

In the morning there was a knock at the door. He figured it was either maid service or one of the pit bosses from downstairs ready to offer him something for free in order to get him playing again. At Sam's Town they would have heard about his win at the Southern Belle—he had learned enough about the casino business to be sure of that. He decided to ignore it, but it came again, loud and persistent. He finally got up and went to the door in his underwear. He wasn't going to get dressed for these bastards.

Opening the door, he froze. Standing there in front of him, with a blazing smile completely unlike any expression he had ever seen on her face before, was Ramona. He stood there wordlessly. What was she doing there?

"Aren't you going to invite me in?" she asked.

It took him a long moment to respond. "Yes, sure, come in," he finally said. "How did you know where I was?"

She walked in and sat on the edge of the bed. "You sure don't know much about casinos," she replied. Then she nodded toward the bag on the TV. "I'll bet you think you won that through skill, don't you?"

Her tone irritated him. "You're goddamn right I do."

She laughed. "Let me show you something." She reached into her purse and pulled out a deck of cards. Fanning through them, she put the ace of spades on top, and then started to deal the cards out on the bed. It seemed like she tossed Taylor the first card, but a six appeared in front of him. "Let me know when you want the ace," she said. He watched her hands carefully as the dealt out the hand and the ace never appeared. It was quite impossible to see that she was doing anything out of the ordinary. On the next hand, he got a ten for his first card. "I'll take the ace now," he said sarcastically, thinking that she had somehow put it on the bottom and there would be some obvious fumbling as she tried to toss it to him. There was no change at all in her fluid movements—just that curious flick of the wrist that seemed nothing but her style—and there it was: the ace of spades. Blackjack.

She looked at his expression and said, "That's nothing. Now let's play through the deck without you telling me what you have, the way it is in the casino." She shuffled the cards and said, "I've got a ten or a five that I can throw you whenever you need it." She dealt a hand and he motioned for a hit. "Wait," she said. "You've got to be as expressive as you normally are at the casino. Pretend you've got two thousand dollars out." Since Taylor had sixteen against her ten up, he let his face take on an expression of resignation over a certain loss as he motioned for the hit. A five appeared in front of him. Twenty one. She turned over twenty. Then she glanced quickly at her watch, a "nervous" gesture he had seen many times before and which now came into focus for the first time.

"Now it isn't quite as good," she said. "I can give you either an eight or a ten. I may have to bust you."

But on the next hand he had eleven against a ten and doubled. She threw him the ten. As she gathered up the discards the deck tilted slightly in her hand. "Now I can give you either an eight or a six," she said. On the next round he motioned for a hit, and she asked, "What do you need?" in the same ironic, playful tone she had used a couple of times yesterday. "Seven," he said, scratching again, and the six appeared. Twenty. A push against her two queens. There was the same tilt of the deck as she gathered up the discards. "Oh, lucky you," she said. "This time you can have an ace." She tossed him the ace, dealt herself an eight, and said, "Now you can have either another six, an eight, or a card that I haven't seen. As I'm sure you know, the count is positive according to High-Opt 2, the count you use." She smiled. Taylor's eyes widened. They hadn't mentioned counting since their first date, never discussed it in detail. "You can either take a fairly sure thing with the eight," she said, "for nineteen, or you can go for a blackjack by gambling on the card I haven't seen."

"I'll take nineteen," he said. The eight appeared beside the ace. She turned over eighteen.

Taylor was astonished. It was part of the record—the criminal record in Vegas—that there were dealers facile enough to deal the second card without it being discernible to the naked eye, but Ramona could deal either from the bottom, the top, or the "second," and she always knew what two cards were, sometimes three, and she could deal him the one he needed with no change at all in the motion of her hands. She could give herself a stiff, she could bust herself, she could keep him from busting, she could give him twenty or blackjack. It dawned on him that she had done so yesterday to the tune of fifty-seven thousand dollars with three cameras trained on her and five or six pit bosses hovering around. The question was why.

"How much of that money do you want?" he asked.

"None," she said. "That was just a sample."

"A sample of what?"

"You and I are going to Vegas. I'm going to get my job back at Caesar's or another of the big casinos on the strip. We'll take down a million dollars in one night. And that's when we'll share."

"Why Vegas? Why not here?"

"Because these low-rent casinos will make you change tables if you start winning big. Usually at ten thousand. The only way we got by with that"—she nodded toward the bag—"is because I had good cards to choose from and it happened so fast. They were getting ready to shut you down when you stopped."

"But why me?" he asked. After all, she had never really seemed to care about him.

"Two reasons: you're a good player who's not afraid to put real money on the table, and then there's another one."

He waited while this woman . . . he could no longer bring himself even to think of her as *Repo* Ramona . . . this woman he had thought emotionless and cold, actually looked bashful and finally managed to say, "It's because I like you more than a little bit."

"I was beginning to wonder, Ramona."

"That's just my way," she said, in that moment looking not quite so hard, not so tough. He brushed the cards from the bed. He held her hands in his, those beautiful, talented hands. It was as if he had opened a door in the west, and limitless vistas of land and sky stretched out before him. Ramona squeezed his hands back. Sometimes a man gambles for money, sometimes for pride, and sometimes, players, for something like vindication.

Less than a week later, Taylor was in his apartment gathering the few things he cared to take with him: shorts and tee shirts, his best suit for the night of the game, the bag of cash. Sarah had nearly everything of value, and she was welcome to all of it. Soon enough he could replace everything. He needed only clothes and money. He phoned Sarah, with whom he had not spoken in a couple of weeks. When she heard his voice, her tone became guarded and distant. He was suddenly fearful and surprised himself by being so. Luckily, he wasn't bringing up "business," just letting her know he would be out of town for a while.

"I want you to keep all these photograph albums while I'm gone. The wedding pictures are in one of them. Mind you, now, I want them when I come back." He hoped she heard this as an oblique compliment: their memories were important to him.

She brought up business: "Taylor, I'm going ahead with the divorce."

"What?" he asked. He was genuinely surprised.

There was a pause. She sighed, presumably at the prospect of trying to justify something that was obvious, and then replied simply: "I've let you go, Taylor."

"Sarah, we need to talk before you do anything final. In any case, I've got to bring these pictures over. We'll talk."

"No, I don't think that's a good idea. And I don't want to keep the pictures. Leave them at your aunt's."

She didn't want him at her house. Suddenly, it was real. He had thought she was quietly sitting at home, humming on standby, waiting for his affair or "crisis" or whatever it was to run its course, and then decide to come back. He had waited too long.

"There's another man," Taylor thought. And simultaneously, the thought crossed his mind that a quick divorce might not be a bad idea. At the moment he was penniless as far as she knew. In the near future that would not be the case—a bad time to start divorce proceedings. Now, it would be a no-fault situation, simple in the doing because he didn't have anything she could take. Sarah had her good points, but generosity in material things was not one of them: he knew she would take him for everything she could get when it came down to it. A quick divorce was the strategic thing. Still, he didn't want it. She had been part of his life for too long. All he could think to say was, "This is stupid."

She did not respond.

He wanted time to think. "I'll talk to you later," he said, and hung up. Sitting there on the futon with his pulse threading through his veins, he knew he had only to call her back and tell her that he loved her. Everything would be as before: familiarity, stability, the days turning to years as he whitewashed yet again the rose-entwined picket fence that was sure to come. But then there was another picture: he saw stacks of thousand dollar orange chips standing out before him in a betting circle, saw Ramona's hands flicking him cards.

Now, a run of luck is by its very nature unlikely, often amazing. Nothing is impossible. There was no reason why Ramona shouldn't give him, say, four ten-thousand dollar blackjacks in a row. He would win sixty thousand dollars before the house even started watching. Sixty thousand dollars in about a minute. Sixty thousand to start. Let Sarah divorce him. The thought made him angry, and the best revenge, after all, is success. He was going to Vegas.

He picked up the telephone and called Stormy's number, which he had gotten out of the Reverend's address book. It was an impulsive act but somehow inevitable.

"Hello." It was a whiskey voice belonging to a middle-aged woman.

"Hello. May I speak with Stormy, please?"

"Hold on." Without taking the phone completely away from her mouth, the woman bellowed for Stormy and Taylor held the receiver away from his ear. He could hear the woman continuing to yell and Stormy's muted voice telling her to "wait a minute, for God's sake." Finally, she picked up the phone.

"Hey, sweetie," he said.

There was a pause. "Uh, hello. How did you get my number?"

"Don't you remember you gave it to me? Stormy, why did you tell the Reverend I made a pass at you."

"You're calling to ask me that? I don't know. Let's say I was confused."

"Well, I'm coming to Vegas. Been on a run of good luck lately. And there's more to come. Do you still want to meet me?"

"A run of luck? How much?

"Enough, little lady. More than enough."

"How much?"

"Enough for us to take a little trip to the Bahamas."

"Well, sure, I'll meet you out here, but you aren't mad at me, are you?"

"I could never stay mad at you. Never. Tell you what. It's going to be a little while before I get there. Do you have e-mail?"

"Yeah, my mother uses a computer for betting the races. I don't know the address though. What's your e-mail address, Mom?"

"You think I can remember that? Are you crazy, girl?" Her voice was as clear to Taylor as it had been when she was yelling for Stormy to come to the phone. He spoke up quickly before a fight could develop. "Don't worry about it. I'll give you mine and when you send something the return address will be on it." He started to give it to her.

"Mom, give me that pencil," she said.

"You're always wanting something," the mother said.

She took down Taylor's address and he had her repeat it to him twice. "Now send something to me quickly because I don't know how much longer I'm going to be here. I can write back and send you the details as they develop. Let me just say this: we'll be lying on a beach drinking margaritas in about a month."

"Really?"

"Really."

He hung up and cursed himself for a fool. But a girl like Stormy . . . and there was something else he needed to work out, something hard. Ramona would have to be told that the Reverend was coming too. And the reason for that . . . Taylor let his eyes wander over the bookcase that had come back home to stay and thought of the not very distant past. He could smell cold steel and hear the snap of bones.

PART 2

♠

"The doors are coming down!" The amplified voice resonated between concrete and steel as cell doors began to roll. Prisoners stepped cautiously out on the "rock," the communal area which the cells surrounded. The breakdown was a mixed blessing. It was good to get out of the cell, but others got out too. And the others had their moods. Some men preferred to stay locked down.

Shelby County Jail, where Taylor had been transported in handcuffs after sheriff's deputies had come to his house and placed him under arrest, and where he would stay until his sentencing because Sarah would not make his bail, was a hodge-podge of criminals, losers, and the unlucky. Dope dealers, Peeping Toms, ersatz pimps, church burglars, pedophiles, card cheaters, robbers, rapists, and murderers mixed uneasily, jockeying for position and forming alliances, generally racial, that might afford safety. Taylor quickly noted that the jailors enjoyed throwing white men with swastika tattoos together with black gangbangers in the same cell block. The air stayed thick with fear and hatred.

Taylor peered cautiously out of his cell and saw the man he had been watching for several days shuffling around the rock on prison-issued flip-flops. Taylor was waiting for a chance to exchange a few words. The man had the air of someone who had been here before and knew the ropes. He walked a circle around the block, and when he reached Taylor, who stood just outside his cell, Taylor said, "Hey there, fellow. Come inside and park it for a minute."

"Not now. I'm riding around. Come on and ride with me."

"My name's Taylor, Taylor Robinson."

They walked a circle, passing the cells and nodding at the men who stayed inside, stepping around those who milled aimlessly on the rock. "They call me Reverend," the man said. "I'm non-denominational. Any creed, sect, or cult will do. I can hear confessions, issue absolution, instruct in techniques of self-denial or scourge, elucidate the Holy Word or the prison sentence. I am ready, willing, and able to perform any type of spiritual service, from beatification to exorcism, for a modest fee. Naturally, in here my fees are even more modest than usual."

There had been a couple of fights at the last breakdown, and it was hot on the rock. Threat hung in the air like a steely mist. As Taylor and the Reverend moved, the mist billowed and swirled into random prisoners. It was hard to tell what effect this might have on a given man, and the uncertainty made Taylor want to be back in his hole. But the Reverend seemed to take it in stride, eliciting a high five from a gangbanger and acknowledging a con here or there. "Gotta test the air, my friend," he said. "I take it you're new to the hospitality of the state."

Taylor looked sidelong at him: "First time I was ever arrested." The Reverend was big, above six feet, with wide shoulders and thick forearms. He had a sort of chiseled lady-killing profile. He was both handsome, Taylor supposed, and hard-looking. There was an intelligence in his wolf-like grey eyes that didn't mix with the hard look. It was unclear yet to Taylor which was veneer.

Taylor had been locked up a week, and had nearly reconciled himself to the fact that Sarah was not going to post his bond. She was insistent over the telephone about his responsibility for the gambling, and if he had lost all his money and committed a crime to get more, he would have to pay the price, not her. If he also lost his job at the college, so be it.

To hell with Sarah. When the next opportunity to use the phone rolled around the following day, he had decided to call his aunt.

The phone had rung with a distant, hollow sound. He had a sense of misgiving even before she answered, and that sense increased when she was silent upon hearing his voice. He listened to a pause, and then, misgiving or not, there was nothing to do but forge ahead.

"Aunt Jane, I need to tell you something. There's been a huge misunderstanding and I'm, uh—

She interrupted him: "I know where you are, Taylor."

"You do? How?"

"Sarah told me."

"She did?"

"Yes, she did. I had no idea that your gambling had gotten this bad."

"Aunt Jane, you know how Sarah exaggerates things."

Taylor heard his aunt say something muffled to someone in the room, then he heard Sarah's voice clearly say, "I don't care."

His aunt uncovered the telephone. "As a matter of fact, she's here right now, Taylor. We've been talking."

"Aunt Jane, I need your help."

"I'm sorry, Taylor. Sarah believes—and I agree—that the best thing for you is to take responsibility for what you've gotten yourself into. And a little time to think about what you're doing to your life isn't a bad idea either. You either get yourself out or stay there until they let you out."

"I can't get myself out. Let me talk to Sarah."

There was a pause and a muffled exchange. "She doesn't want to talk to you, Taylor."

"Let me talk to her!" Were there words in the language sharper than fangs?

A guard overheard Taylor's tone and walked toward him. "Time's up," the guard said.

"Just a minute, for God's sake," Taylor said. "Aunt Jane, please"—the guard grabbed the phone out of Taylor's hand. "Time's up," he said, and slammed down the receiver.

Taylor would later understand clearly what he could not then, even in his anger, allow himself to realize: Sarah's refusal to help and her blocking his last alternative was the real divorce. Everything after that was just details. At the moment, his immediate problem was in finding a way to survive in jail until he could beat his charge. Surely, he would stay here only until his trial came up, and then walk. No judge would actually sentence him. It was simply a matter of making it for a couple of weeks without getting his teeth knocked out.

The divide in the jail was race, and that divide could hardly have been worse. Taylor had yet to see the Grand Canyon, which would have given him a metaphor for the distance between the races. If there was any accord on the outside, fictive or otherwise, it did not show itself inside these walls. Blacks were openly antagonistic toward whites. Whites were conspiratorial against blacks. An odd Muslim or a few Hispanics here or there simply emphasized the insular nature of the city. Within an atmosphere of simmering hatred that sometimes broke out into open skirmishes, one jockeyed for safety within the confines of one's own race, hopefully hooking up with a group that was neutral in stance but violent in defense of its members, should the need arise.

Taylor saw the Reverend's eyes harden. His face turned to stone in an instant and it was as if someone else was standing there. He was watching a line of gangbangers form outside of little Jinx's cell. About eighteen, Jinx was a kid the Reverend had befriended who was now being forced to "give" away his cakes, cookies, and cigarettes, his zuzus, wham-whams, and squares.

As messed up a kid as lived to steal, Jinx had reputedly been normal until a few years back, according to the Reverend, when a car wreck left him with just enough life to last too long and not enough sense to do it with. He seemed to have lost the part of his brain that understood ownership. Now, whenever Jinx saw something that sparkled, it didn't necessarily register that it wasn't his. The most recent sparkling thing was a neighbor's Cadillac that Jinx hot-wired, then cool-rode for days and nights without sleep, smoking awesome amounts of reefer, he said, chugging only the best whiskey, and impressing every kind of girl. Then he came around to crashing, so geeked out that he parked the car directly in front of his parents' house, two doors down from its owner, and went inside and slept until the cops came for him.

"That kid needs to be in some kind of hospital," the Reverend said.

When Jinx had nothing left, and the last gangbangers in the line turned away muttering, he darted out of his cell and came towards the Reverend. "Jinx," the Reverend said, "next time you get the police to lock your cell back after the breakdown. You come down to my cell."

"Right, Reverend. Then they can't take any more of my stuff."

From that point, the Reverend's number three cell became established as a kind of foxhole, and a number of prisoners would congregate there at the breakdown. The days passed. Jinx continued to have trouble. "Reverend, the man in the cell next to me ought to be in the sissy block."

"Why is that?" Taylor asked.

Jinx described the act he thought had been suggested, and the older prisoners laughed. "What's so funny?" he asked.

"Little brother," the Reverend said, "that man likes baseball, but he pitches, he don't catch." Jinx's face twisted in disgust. "But don't worry about it, buddy. Ain't nobody gonna do nothing or take nothing from you no more."

A new man had just come up from three cigaretteless days on the lower level, where he had been since his arrest. He was about thirty, heavy-set, wearing a fifty-cent cap that sported a confederate flag.

"That rebel hat's not gonna make you very popular around here," Taylor said. He wondered why the police hadn't confiscated the cap, then thought again.

"So what?" the man said. "This won't either." He pushed up the sleeve of his green jail-issued pullover to show a tattoo that read "Iron Horsemen/Enforcer" above a swastika. The Iron Horsemen were a local motorcycle gang; one of their "enforcers" was probably particularly vicious. The quality of the clique in cell three was improving. There was a potential problem, however, revolving around the matter of literacy.

"I'm not sure that's gonna impress anybody," Taylor said. "Most of them can't read it."

"I'll read it to them," the Enforcer said. Taylor wondered how long this bravado would last. Still, muscle for an outlaw motorcycle gang couldn't hurt.

"Have a cigarette, rap," Taylor said. The Enforcer gulped down smoke viciously, exhaled with a sigh and watched the smoke drift into stark light.

"What's your charge?" he asked Taylor.

"Bogus credit card."

"And yours?" he said to the Reverend.

"More sin than crime, my friend, if you understand the distinction. That is to say, the law is holding me for grand larceny and attempted murder"—he snorted derisively—"but my sin was to come between a woman and the man to whom God had joined her."

The Enforcer blinked. "Come again?" he said.

"I was the pastor of a small congregation in rural Arkansas. I'm a man of the cloth, as you've probably gathered. Well, one of the young mothers in the flock sought solace for marital difficulties, and I provided it."

The Reverend paused and leered. "She was both excellent in her frustration, my friends, and well-solaced, if I do say so myself." He paused as the snickers subsided, then drew a breath to continue: "Unfortunately, she was also indiscreet. Her husband came pounding on my door in the middle of the night, carrying a club and backed by a couple of other hillbillies, probably relatives from the same shallow gene pool. I was forced to defend myself. Needless to say, I defended myself with a weapon against these yokels carrying baseball bats. They scattered into the woods with .38 slugs whizzing past their ears." Taylor, Jinx, and the Enforcer laughed.

"As I took stock of the situation, I considered the likelihood that they would be back before dawn with guns of their own. I had no choice but to take it on the lam, as many another man of God has done before me, and unfortunately neglected to remember that I had the monthly church receipts in my pocket. When the law caught up with me in Memphis and I was brought here, I got wind of these rather serious charges. But who's to say that it wasn't an honest mistake?—as a pastor I'm entrusted with the church offerings—and who can say that I didn't shoot to miss?"

"Hell, Reverend," Jinx said, "who's to say you weren't shooting blanks just to scare them off?"

"Exactly, son." The Reverend leaned back on his elbows, looking pensive. "In point of fact, that's exactly what I was shooting. My gun was loaded with blanks."

"Can you prove that?" the Enforcer asked.

"Can they prove otherwise?" the Reverend answered, looking smugly at them all. "It's just a matter of getting them to break it down to misdemeanor charges. I can't take another felony."

In the ensuing discussion Taylor came to understand that, should the state pursue a felony conviction against the Reverend, he could face prosecution under the Habitual Criminal Act, a plan reserved for three-time losers. Like a frequent flyer bonus. Thirty years.

"Can you feature getting thirty years for defending yourself with a harmless bluff . . . or a spell of absent-mindedness?" the Reverend asked.

No, nobody could.

"But these bastards can do anything," the Reverend continued. "I had a buddy in Parchman got the bitch for violation of probation. He told the judge, "Your honor, I can't do thirty years." The judge said, "Tell you what, son. Just do all of it you can."

"Catch a hole!"

It was mother, calling them home, and everyone shuffled out of number three toward his own cell. Jinx's cell was on the far end, and two gangbangers joined him, one on each side, as he shuffled along. Taylor watched the Reverend watch Jinx as he entered his cell and handed out a pack of cigarettes. Taylor watched the Reverend stiffen as he realized someone other than Taylor was watching him. Turning, the Reverend looked across the block at three sullen, taunting faces. They didn't want anybody protecting Jinx.

"Doors coming down!"

The steel doors rolled, then locks cracked in sequence down the line like gunshots from a passing car. For a moment there was a resonant silence as everyone breathed in his own separate misery, then hoots and jeers erupted from everywhere at once.

"Officer! Officer! I need a officer to perform a homoseckshul act!"

"One Cell, I'm getting out tomorrow, so what's that number?"

"What number?"

"Number of that pig you call a wife."

Sounds of snorting, blowing, howls echoing from concrete and steel. Thirteen and Fourteen Cell, directly across from Taylor, were carrying on a discussion of legal and theological import at the top of their lungs.

"Do you believe a man can breed with a animal?"

"Sho, man. That be why God come down on it so deep."

"It ain't impossible?"

"Telling you now it ain't. There's two things you can't mess with: a animal or a angel."

"Well, if I ever gets a chance with a angel, I'll sure enough see what's that like. Know what I'm saying?"

"No you ain't neither. You mess with a angel, you be doing more time than this little deuce you got for messing with that ho. You be doing eternity, Jack. Double, triple life."

"What about a animal? They got a charge on that?"

"Man, don't you know they got a charge on everything they wants to have a charge on? But that ain't just exactly why you don't wanna do it. Say you gets a cow or a sheep pregnant. What kinda child that gonna be? I'm asking you. What kinda child? And who gonna pay the child support?"

The long hours before breakfast loomed up before Taylor like the barrel of a .38. He lay down on the iron bunk's stiff plastic mattress that measured 72" by 24" by 4" and did not sleep. He was still struggling to find a way to accept the fact that his wife had left him here, and then he was thinking about the game. Hands good and bad, well-played and otherwise, ran through his mind. It was something other than Sarah to think about. Sarah, who was perhaps even now luxuriating between silk sheets in a four poster bed, and maybe not doing so alone.

The hours somehow passed, and after a 3:00 a.m. breakfast of soggy toast and gravy, they were locked down for a few hours more before both Taylor and the Reverend were called to court. A few men were awake to hear them called out, and wished them luck. Jinx had probably *waited* up in order to call from the far end of the block: "Time served, Reverend! Don't take nothing but time served!"

This was their third trip to court; most indigent inmates get at least that many. The first appearance had been a preliminary hearing which hardly required the presence of the accused. There, bond was set at the judge's whim, informed or not. Bedraggled men unable to make bond were ushered into the rear of the courtroom after as many as four days alone in a cell on the lowest level of the Justice Complex without bathing or shaving, eating exactly three sandwiches (peanut butter or unidentifiable meat on dry white bread) a day. The second appearance, about a week later, was another formality for the appointment of an attorney. The third time around, men were offered a "deal," and if they decided to take it, were sentenced.

Because he had never spoken with his attorney since she was appointed to represent him, the Reverend had no idea what his deal might be. And because the judge was apparently still laboring under the delusion that Taylor could make bail, he had yet to be appointed an attorney. Taylor almost took that as a good sign. Maybe he wouldn't need one. His crime, in the context of his law-abiding life, had been aberrant and impulsive. Surely he wouldn't actually do any time. He merely needed a chance to explain things to the judge.

In the corridor outside of the cell block, they were strip-searched. The guard missed the two cigarettes hidden in Taylor's hair, thanks kindly. Now it would be a matter of finding someone in the holding tank below who had smuggled in a match. With fifteen other men from various cell blocks on the floor, they were herded into a cage that measured about six by six, and there they waited for thirty minutes. Taylor could have chinned himself on the breath of the glassy-eyed wino beside him.

The door opened at last, and everyone began riding the escalators downstairs. Guards behind thick glass in little rooms that resembled airplane cockpits with all their instruments and dials occasionally offered up bored glances to make certain no one simply stopped. There was, of course, nowhere to go but down.

They went down to tunnels below street-level where they were put into a holding cell with about fifty other men. There, they waited for about two hours, listening to the usual arguments about which pimp had the most whores. At last their names were called together, and the Reverend and Taylor trudged along maze-like corridors to get to another, smaller holding tank. There, packed wall to wall again, they waited.

A kid about twenty was hunkering in the corner in the official posture of narcotics withdrawal: bent at the waist, arms crossed and hugging his shoulders. At first, Taylor took him for a junkie coming up from the lower level for his first court appearance, then recognized him from upstairs. No, the kid was more lunatic than junkie. Taylor watched him scope out the Reverend.

"They told me you were a priest. Are you a priest?" he asked in a weird, guttural whisper.

"I am a non-denominational man of the cloth," the Reverend said.

"Can you hear a confession?"

"Can you get me a honeybun at the next store call?"

The kid nodded, so the Reverend replied, "Okay, come into the confessional."

The two walked behind the metal partition that separated the toilet from the room. A dozen men stared wordlessly, watching through the space where the partition did not reach the floor. As they could see from his shoes, the Reverend seated himself on the toilet. The kid sat on the floor, not facing him, as is appropriate.

"Father, I have sinned . . ."

Taylor and the others listened in silence as a low but perfectly clear voice enunciated and presumably expiated various loathsome sexual acts he had been required to perform by way of initiation into a motorcycle club, including French kissing an Irish setter, an act that really tore him up.

"But did you enjoy it?" the Reverend asked in psychotherapeutic tones.

"No, father. Not for a minute."

"Then you are absolved without so much as a Hail Mary."

"Thank you, father."

"But tell me, my son, what's the charge that brought you here?"

"Robbery."

"Would you care to confess that?"

"No."

"Nevertheless, you are absolved without a single Our Father."

At that point Taylor heard their names being called yet again, and stuck his head around the partition. "They're calling us, Reverend," he said, and if the Reverend heard anything at all in the way Taylor said his name, his expression conveyed that he found such irony unwarranted.

They entered the courtroom from the rear alongside and very much beneath the judge, then jockeyed for a seat on a bench where nine men sat hip to hip. Taylor blinked out at the people in the courtroom and realized he had been locked up long enough to think that they wore an amazing variety of clothes. At first he felt as if he were on stage, but then realized that the spectators' glances were directed above him at the judge. It was as if he had turned around in a theatre and saw everyone staring over him with slack mouths, a bovine glaze across their eyes.

The Reverend's lawyer, a singularly unattractive woman with sweat seeping through the armpits of her cheap suit, approached the bench and asked two or three men whether they were Danny Askander before he got her attention. She stepped over to him and whispered confidentially, "The D. A.'s offering eleven months and twenty nine days. No felony."

"The last part's good, but what's the charge? Defending myself? Taking money that was entrusted to me? Money that was neither mine nor theirs but the Lord's?"

The woman's face contorted in disgust. "And I suppose the Lord wanted you to come to Memphis and spend it on a skid row binge."

At that moment the bailiff called his name and pointed contemptuously to where the Reverend should stand. He looked at his lawyer, the D. A., and the judge. Time for a decision. He motioned to his lawyer, and Taylor heard him say, "Tell the D. A. I'm not even thinking about eleven twenty nine on this jive charge."

His lawyer took more than a moment to compose herself, then said, "Your honor, my client requests a continuance in order to consider the D. A.'s offer."

"Next Tuesday, nine o'clock," the judge said. "Next, please."

Taylor's name was called and he presented himself, trying to appear just a bit bemused by this misunderstanding that had landed him in jail. It could not be said that the judge responded in kind. She looked at him with the deadpan expression that Taylor was beginning to recognize as common to all officials of criminal justicedom, an expression that might take a certain pleasure in affecting others but was not itself to be affected. Later, in prison, he would notice the same phenomenon in guards who would jovially tell him jokes, chuckle heartily when he laughed, then roll their eyes and look away if he began to tell one.

Now, the judge started into the bond routine again, as she had last week. She was apparently unable to believe that a man with Taylor's job was unable to make bond. It wasn't enough for her to establish his indigence; she wanted him to tell her why. As far as Taylor was concerned, it was none of her business.

"You have no family at all?"

Last week, Taylor had decided to tell her this rather than go into the humiliating fact that neither his wife nor his aunt would make his bail. Seeming to sense his discomfort, the judge became more animated. This was fun. "What happened to that Cadillac you used to drive? Did you sell it?"

The courtroom tittered appreciatively. Here was a judge who could make a joke. Taylor responded: "Actually, I misplaced it."

"Why didn't you look for it?"

"Because someone else misplaced it before I did." Now Taylor had made a joke. The prisoners on the bench chuckled under their breath. The judge's face got a little stonier, her lips a little tighter. She put an end to the fun and appointed Taylor an attorney. He got the sweaty woman who didn't recognize her clients.

Once he had become cynical about the so-called justice system, which took about a week, Taylor began to wonder why the prosecution would "make an offer" to indigent defendants. After all, what did he or the others have to bargain with? Then he understood: there was always the remote but conceivable chance that one of them might be stupid enough to want a trial. This was the worst possible scenario in terms of work and expense over the penniless cretin, who might be innocent of the charge at hand but wasn't innocent of being broke and a pain in the ass. Thus, judges, district attorneys, and public defenders worked together to pressure the defendant into pleading guilty and going somewhere, anywhere, else.

Yet the D. A.'s and the court-appointed defense attorneys were supposed to be adversaries, right? Hardly. Taylor realized this as he considered the role of the court-appointed attorney. These low-level lawyers were appointees of a main Public Defender, who was himself an appointee of the County Board of Commissioners. These people were paid a flat salary regardless of the outcome of cases. They worked with the same D. A.'s and judges everyday. Together, this triad worked as efficiently as possible in the vastly overcrowded criminal justice system, which threatened to devolve from its present near-unintelligibility into a completely arbitrary state, to get prisoners out of the county jail and into a prison where they would be someone else's problem.

There was little if any incentive for a public defender to do a good job other than idealism or the possibility that incompetence might come to someone's attention. Idealism wore thin in the justice system as quickly as sweat soaked through a polyester suit, and the Public Defender's taking note of a poor performance would be drawn far more readily by ineptitude in courtroom procedure, which the boss might find out about on the occasion of an appeal, than by a lack of fervor in developing a case for the client. The surest way a court-appointed attorney could draw criticism of "courtroom procedure" was to have any courtroom procedure, to be a genuine advocate of his client's rights and an adversary to the D. A. And the surest way to interrupt the basic function of the system, which was to move bodies expediently to prison, was to introduce evidence suggesting, say, the need for a trial.

When Taylor arrived back on the floor, the Reverend was still standing around waiting for the guard who would search them before they were let back into the cell block. A guard finally appeared, saying to Taylor, "Turn around and spread 'em, honky." At least he knew where this particular guard's sympathies were not.

When they were let in, the block was strangely quiet. No one called to ask how it went for them. "What's up?" the Reverend called from within his cell.

There was a long silence, then the Enforcer answered from down the block: "Jinx had a little trouble after you left this morning."

"Jinx, how ya doing, buddy?" the Reverend called out.

"He ain't here, Reverend."

"Where is he?"

"They took him to the hospital."

During this exchange, the men responsible for sending him there were listening, and both Taylor and the Reverend knew it.

"Who did it?" Taylor asked automatically.

Fourteen Cell from down the block cut in: "What you wanna know who did it for, boy?"

Thirteen Cell: "You gonna do something about it, trick?"

"You should just leave that kid alone."

Too late, Taylor realized that, by jailhouse standards, he was interfering in someone else's business. He had just taken a side. Now silence stretched out of his cell like a sentence for The Bitch.

A few days later, on commissary night, there was a line outside of Jinx's cell.

"Gimme a cake."

"Gimme a zuzu."

"Gimme some squares. I don't want that roll-up. I want Kools."

Jinx handed them the stuff with his good arm. The other was in a cast. They had caught his arm, pulled it through the bars, and broken it. Now he gave them what they wanted.

There was no day or night in Shelby County Jail. One could get a glimpse of sunlight through two thicknesses of tinted glass at the far end of the block, but none of the prisoners paid any attention. What difference did it make? It was morning when there was watery coffee with the meal. The passage of time is normally judged by a succession of events, frames of mind. Here, nothing ever changed, really. The tension stayed constant, punctuated only when it was ratcheted up by a burst of terror. Taylor and the Reverend had been there a month. It might have been a day or a year.

They found some relief playing chess on the board Taylor made from paper. The pieces were paper squares with their identity inked on. Soon enough, Taylor was unaware that it wasn't a real set. One day, the Reverend beat him. Taylor asked him how. The Reverend answered, "When you moved your knight here—he picked up the taken piece—rather than here, that left me free to sacrifice this bishop—again, he repositioned the piece—so I could come here with my queen." He was recreating neither the endgame nor the opening but something that had happened mid-game, about fifteen or twenty moves before. At that moment, Taylor was fairly certain that he would never beat the Reverend again. And something else occurred to him.

"Do you want to learn to play blackjack?"

"I guess I know how . . . it's a simple game."

"I mean how to really play it. Play it to win."

"Well, sure. What's your angle?"

"Two good players together are better than one, for reasons you'll understand later. I'll find us some cards."

"Fine with me."

The Reverend leaned back against the wall and a shadow passed across his face. Taylor knew what he was thinking about, and said, "You gotta be sure you don't mess around with this charge long enough for them to decide to return a felony indictment."

"Would you take eleven twenty-nine for defending yourself?" the Reverend asked. He had apparently decided to forget about the money thing.

"Can't say that I would, Reverend. But I wouldn't do thirty years either."

The Reverend pondered for a moment. "If I could just get a felony year without a felony charge, I'd take it."

"Right. Go to the state pen and get out as soon as you get there."

Tennessee prisons were under a federal court order to release fifty more prisoners each month than they took in. As a result, many nonviolent offenders were getting time cuts. Of course, it was also questionable whether the Reverend would be seen as nonviolent or not. "I just hope," he said, nodding towards the open cell door, "that things don't get so bad here I have to take a bum deal to get to the penal farm."

Since Thirteen Cell had held Jinx's arm through the bars of his cell and Fourteen Cell had pulled it the wrong way, the atmosphere on the block had been thick, real thick. At Taylor's suggestion, Jinx now had begun to stay locked down twenty-four seven so no one could come into his cell and take anything. Taylor immediately went to the Reverend's cell when the doors came down. His own cell would be a bad place to get cornered in alone. Taylor had stood on his bunk, measuring kicks at the eye level of someone entering the cell. At meals, he had collected a styrofoam cup full of pepper a little at a time. Something for their eyes. He had a shank made from three ball-point pens melted together and sharpened to a point on the concrete floor. Maybe he could bluff someone with it. A kick, pepper, and a bluff.

Suddenly, four or five gangbangers were standing outside of the Reverend's cell. Adrenalin pumped in Taylor's veins like a bad drug. Fourteen Cell looked in and his voice was flat, unconditional: "Don't be talking to your little roadie no more. Don't say nothing. We don't want to see his cell locked no more."

Then a strange dialogue ensued between the men outside, as if they were discussing the weather: "I don't believe you can hit him as hard as I can."

"I bet I can knock him all the way across the rock. Knock him out."

"And if it takes more than three punches, you owe me a honeybun."

The lockdown came like a governor's reprieve. Taylor was back in his cell, and the adrenalin had just eased off, leaving its brassy aftertaste, when a guard called him: "K4, you've got a lawyer visit." Taylor shuffled out when the door rolled. An offer?

Downstairs, he entered a featureless room containing a table, two plastic chairs, and the lawyer. There was a metallic quality to the light and a very slight antiseptic odor issued either from the room or the woman. She raised her face, registered his presence with emotionless eyes, and went back to shuffling papers, unhurried by his silent gaze. After a long silence she finally said, without looking up, "I've got some good news for you, Johnson."

"My name's Robinson."

She went back to shuffling papers and Taylor had a feeling she would not have good news for him.

"Here we are. The D. A. doesn't intend to amend your charge of grand larceny. But he won't pursue the maximum sentence. How does two years sound to you?"

His feeling was right, right with a vengeance. "Two years! I won't take it. I didn't even know that card didn't belong to me. I had it in my wallet, yes, but I had forgotten that it wasn't mine. It was just an impulse thing. I pulled it out and the number was written on it. I had thought about using it, sure, but changed my mind. I'd had it for six months . . ."

"Hold it. What do you mean you won't take it? You've got to take it. You're caught. Take the two years and be glad it's not three."

"Ma'am, this is a first offense. I've got no criminal record."

"You've got a D. U. I. and possession of marijuana from '77."

Taylor remembered the gleeful cop smiling and swinging the marijuana in his hand that he had just taken out of Taylor's glove compartment. He had been pulled over for running a yellow light and he had been drinking. He plead guilty to the D. U. I. and *nolo contendre* to the marijuana charge, which at the time he had been given to understand was something akin to the charges being dropped. It all seemed like ancient history.

"That counts?"

The woman blew through dilated nostrils and allowed herself a small show of emotion. "Take a walk," she said.

Back upstairs, he alternately stood and lay on his bunk, waiting for the breakdown. Somehow, it was clear what was going to happen. It was time. When the doors were about to roll, Jinx, who apparently sensed something also, yelled for the guard to leave his cell locked. It was a different guard, either new, uninformed, or even more malicious than the other one. He looked down the cell block at Jinx, nodded, and Jinx's door rolled open along with the rest.

For a moment, there was silence. Taylor decided to stay in his hole rather than cross the rock to the Reverend's cell. There was a commotion at the other end and he peered out. Thirteen Cell was forcing a pack of cigarettes out of Jinx's useable hand. Taylor swung out of his cell before he had time to think about it and said, "You bastards leave the kid alone."

The rock was instantly silent. Here it was. Let it come down. Three dark men turned together, their movements as stylized as a dance. There was no surprise in their cold eyes as they started toward Taylor's cell. Two held their hands behind their backs, one in the crotch of his pants, poses that indicated, or bluffed, the presence of weapons.

Taylor backed into his cell and stood on the bunk with his cup of pepper in his hand, waiting. Then he saw the Reverend coming across the rock. "You might need a little help, buddy," the Reverend said as he ducked into the cell. "We both might. If they think they can talk to us like they've been doing, they'll try to punk us out. We could be in Jinx's position next. Or worse." He looked down at his flip-flops. "Too bad we don't have any shit-kicking boots." He stood against the wall on the other side of the door from Taylor, who tossed him the pen shank.

When the first one peeked in the Reverend stabbed him in the face. The shank held up, punctured the man's cheek, and slid down his teeth.

Then they were both swinging wildly and the Reverend was knocked toward the rear of the cell. The second followed and, as the third was coming in, Taylor tossed the pepper with a backhanded gesture. Few things more unlikely have ever worked as well.

This world is graced with any number of painful things. For instance, Taylor had caught a glimpse of a pale, taught-faced junkie kicking a methadone habit cold in the hole at Shelby County Jail while the jailors taunted him, and it did not look good. He had heard a young boy being gang-raped in the next cell block, screaming "Help! Help! Help!" with the same frantic rhythm as a barking dog, and that had seemed worse. Taylor and the Reverend together could have listed many types of graces along these lines, especially since the Reverend was a religious man who had devoted a lot of time and thought to the mysterious ways of our Maker and his whimsical means of self-expression toward those created in His image, but Taylor seemed to have found one of the sharpest thorns; judging from Fourteen Cell's reaction, a couple of ounces of pepper in each eye yields a singular pain.

His face was toward Taylor but his eyes were cut toward the Reverend in the rear of the cell, so he didn't see it coming and he didn't even blink. Pepper splashed in his face and he clutched convulsively at his eyes as if he had seen Taylor's lawyer naked, and while he was blind Taylor kicked him in the head, knocking him hard against the bars. Taylor stomped on his shoulders, knocking him to the floor, and there was a solid thud, like an arrow hitting a target, when Taylor jumped down and kicked him in the face.

The Reverend was backed into the rear of the cell, screaming, and Taylor started toward him. Then there was a hand on his shoulder spinning him around, and he barely had time to register on the dark fist before it caught him between the eyes. Light faded to dark, then exploded in a literal rendering of cartoon stars as he was hit a second time. Perspective deepened, then snapped back, and he was on his hands and knees scrambling out of the cell. Through the roar in his head he could still hear screams coming from the rear of the cell. For a moment before the kicks started he lay on the floor of the rock and saw the Reverend fall backwards out of the cell. Then there were five or six men surrounding them, kicking from whichever direction they tried to move. A bone snapped audibly, whether his or the Reverend's Taylor did not know. After a while, the two quit moving and only flinched slightly at the intermittent kicks. Like very drunk men in a bar brawl, they were punching bags.

When Taylor and the Reverend got back from the hospital after a couple of days they were put into adjacent cells in a different cell block. They were moved possibly because the guards didn't care to deal with dead bodies—all that paperwork—which there would certainly have been after another such fight. Both of them were in severe pain, and any medication was out of the question. The Reverend had a broken collar bone. Taylor had three broken ribs which would hurt him for six months.

The two were going to court again today. "I'm ready to deal," the Reverend said, speaking around, as it were, the concrete wall that separated them. "We've got to get out of here. This little cell block change don't mean nothing. We can't stay here any longer without being able to protect ourselves."

The doors rolled. It was a long trip down. They waited about five hours in the holding cells before getting into the courtroom. Their lawyer looked toward the group of not very prepossessing prisoners as if straining, as ever, for recognition. She approached the Reverend. "The offer's still eleven twenty nine at the penal farm," she whispered. "Be glad

I got you a misdemeanor."

"You didn't get it. I got it," the Reverend said flatly.

Her conspiratorial smile faded to contempt, and she jabbed a piece of paper at him. "Sign this." The Reverend signed with his left hand and was called to the bench. The judge put on her stern face, like an amateur actress getting into character. She was going to emote.

"Mr. Askander, you're getting a very light sentence considering other alternatives the district attorney had, and I think you know what I mean. You do understand the implications of your ever coming before this court again with a felony charge, don't you?"

"Yes, your honor."

"Let me make it very clear to you. If I see you again, I will recommend prosecution under the Habitual Criminal Act. Now, I can't stop you from pretending to be a minister"—

"Your honor, I am a man of the cloth."

The judge snapped her gavel down and the sound echoed through the courtroom. "Don't tempt me!" she said. "I can't stop you from this charade unless you happen to misrepresent yourself to a legitimate organization by saying that you're ordained. If that happens, you'll be charged with fraud."

"Your honor, if I may say so, we are ordained only by God, and that's the only claim I've ever made."

The judge snorted. "Make sure it stays that way, Mr. Askander." She turned toward the court reporter. "Eleven months twenty nine days. Shelby County Correctional Facility. Next."

The Reverend was escorted out and Taylor's name was called. He stood before the bench with his head swimming, realizing that he wasn't really hearing the judge's words. He did, however, hear her tone: the false, fruity tone of a schoolteacher about to administer a paddling. He watched her mouth move like a mechanical doll's and was suddenly transfixed by the realization that all of them on trial were, pure and simple, not people at all but props in a play. He looked at the floor.

There was a lot of conferring between his lawyer and the D. A. Then she came back offering nine months at the Penal Farm like it was a birthday present. Taylor took it. He was ready to deal. He and the Reverend would ride away from Shelby County Jail late that night.

He was ushered back to the holding cell where the Reverend still waited. "Nine months," he said, and the Reverend nodded. Then there was silence. After a moment, Taylor said, "I wonder how Jinx is making it."

"I talked to a man from K block in the chow hall," the Reverend said. "Jinx got a couple of years, and he's already gone to the penitentiary."

"Figure he'll make it?"

"More likely there than here, in some ways. They got a semblance of a mental health unit. Of course, Jinx probably won't get in it."

"I've got to say something, Reverend. I appreciate what you did. Helping me, I mean. I guess I've never really seen anything like that, not when the stakes were that high, not when it amounted to anything."

The Reverend hitched up his jeans. "Well, there ain't no person that's all bad, buddy. You should know that. Not even a habitual criminal. And no person that's all good." He paused, looking pensive, like he was about to make a confession. "Not even the most dedicated man of the cloth."

Taylor laughed. The Reverend looked perplexed.

Some time later, players, Taylor would remember laughing.

A few hours to go in Shelby County Jail. Taylor looked around in his cell. He wondered how long he had been here. It didn't matter. It was over. He was getting out alive, with all his teeth, and the penal farm was said to be safer. Suddenly, a voice called out: "Five Cell! We know you and your partner shanked a brother over in K block. You bitches gonna pay for that."

Taylor answered, "We didn't shank anybody."

"We know what you did, bitch."

The Reverend called out, "He can't fight, man. He's got broken ribs."

"He gonna have worse than that when these doors come down. And you too."

Taylor eased up to the bars and looked across at sullen faces as far down the block as he could see. So that was how it was. The air was thick. There was nothing to do now but stand up and get ready. The doors were coming down. He waited.

Before the cell doors rolled a guard swung open the main door to the block and yelled, "Danny Askander, Taylor Robinson. Get your stuff. Going to the farm." Only their two doors opened, and then they were skittering out of the block, looking back at taunting faces.

Soon enough they were riding in a prison van through the night on streets that had become curiously unfamiliar to Taylor. They passed restaurants and theatres where, a month previously, he had been free to go. Now they were distant paradises for the privileged. His life was different now, and he knew it always would be.

The penal farm was not a boy's school, but it was not as bad as the jail. He and the Reverend did their time, and as the months passed Taylor taught him how to play blackjack, and in the teaching learned more than he had ever thought possible. After five months Taylor no longer needed cards. Like a musician reading a score and hearing the music in his head, or a chess player playing blind, the cards themselves had become unnecessary. The Reverend would list fifty or fifty one cards as quickly as he could speak them, then ask, "Which card did I leave out?" Taylor had no problem with the question.

This ability was similar to that of, say, a young man who is very interested in baseball and can "call" a game after it is over. He knows that the second batter in the bottom of the third inning grounded out to shortstop on a three and two count. He knows, in fact, what happened on every pitch in the game. Essentially, he replays the game in his mind, and this is what Taylor did with the "deck."

At first, he simply counted the cards. But his count, Hi-Opt 2, was not interested, as it were, in precise cards but the ratio of "good" cards to "bad" cards. Using Hi-Opt 2, Taylor could sometimes know, depending on what cards the Reverend called out, that the last two or three cards were tens; he could sometimes say that the last three were all fours or fives, but sometimes the count would allow him to be no more precise than to say that the last card was either a two, three, six, or seven. Taylor found that with a single deck he no longer needed a count to know what the last card was. If he thought of the "deck" that the Reverend was telling him as thirteen sets of four, it had become possible for him to keep up with each set and "discard" it mentally as the Reverend began to come toward the end. "That's the last seven," he would think. "That's the last ace." As the sets dwindled, it was easier to do. When the Reverend finished, Taylor would think that a five remained, then review the picture that had formed in his mind as the Reverend called the cards. Yeah, only three fives had been called. Often, the Reverend would try to pull a fast one analogous to what a crooked casino might do: add a five or other small card to the deck. At first, Taylor was fooled. Soon he would notice most of the time. After some months, he always caught it.

From the start, Sarah wrote four or five times a week and came to see him on every visitor's day. He tried to bury his resentment but it was hard. He would return to the cell block from a visit shaking his head, not knowing how to feel.

After one visit, the Reverend asked, "I don't get this, buddy. If your wife had made your bail and you had had a half-decent lawyer, you wouldn't be doing any time at all on that little credit card bullshit. So why does she come to see you if she put you here?"

"She doesn't think she put me here, Reverend. She thinks I put myself here."

"Yes, but she could have gotten you out of it."

"I know." It was a hard thing for Taylor to know.

"I mean, no offense, buddy, but it looks to me like your wife's your worst enemy."

"She probably thinks this is what I need."

The Reverend looked around the block. "She must be fucking crazy."

"Well, she's different, Reverend. She's different."

"And you're going back to her when you get out of here? After what she did to you? Why?"

For a moment Taylor almost said that he loved her, but he knew how it would sound. "We have a life together. A nice house. Cats."

"Man, you don't even have a job because of her."

When he thought about things that way, and he often did, Taylor felt his face get hot with anger. Maybe he should tell her not to come see him, tell her to kiss off, tell her he wanted a divorce. But that was the kind of news that came from the outside of a prison in.

The months passed. The Reverend came to understand that they could beat the game, and planned to join Taylor when his hitch was up. They would need a stake. There was Taylor's retirement . . . and the Reverend's part? With a malicious grin he told Taylor that he hadn't exactly spent all of the, ahem, church's building fund. "We'll do a little building of our own, buddy."

When Taylor got out (a couple of months before the Reverend), Sarah was there to pick him up. Driving home a free man, he thought for a moment that he could forgive and forget. But he never thought for a moment that he would stop playing blackjack. And when he didn't, Sarah left.

PART 3

♠

"That's out of the question," Ramona said. "If the Reverend comes, I'm not going to do it. I don't trust him, and we don't need him."

"I can't leave my partner behind on something like this. Anyway, you don't understand. You can trust him."

"He's a lowlife, and he's a gun nut. A habitual criminal, for God's sake. Are you crazy?"

"Ramona, please. It's a long story. He showed me the ropes in prison. Maybe I wouldn't have survived without him. Now that we're out, and I'm in a position to return the favor . . ."

"No. I won't do it. If he knows about it, we're just that much more likely to get caught. You haven't told him about me, have you?"

"No, of course not. I wanted to clear it with you first."

"Well, it is definitely *not* cleared. I wouldn't put it above him to brag about the prospect."

"Ramona, you don't know him."

"I know the type. He's dangerous and he'll ruin everything."

Taylor stopped and considered for a moment. What would the Reverend do if he left for Las Vegas? The Reverend had no one to help him and his job at the warehouse had come to an end. Suddenly, Taylor came up with an idea. "What if he comes with us but doesn't know what's going on? What if I just share some of my winnings with him, and then you and I leave him there with a stake? At least he'll have something to roll with."

Ramona thought for a moment. "If it's got to be, I suppose I don't have any problem with that. As long as he never knows and isn't there the night we take it down. I mean it, Taylor. He *cannot* be there when we take it down."

Taylor was puzzled. "If he doesn't know what's happening, what difference does it make?"

"It'll be written all over his face that the three of us know each other. There are lots of ways he could screw it up, and I'm sure he could think of some we can't. Look—a year from now I really don't want to be telling my cell mate that the reason I'm there is because my boyfriend had to let a third person in on the deal. And I don't want to be telling that same story in the same cell ten years from now."

"Ten years?"

"You don't think they would take this lightly, do you? The money in Nevada comes from casinos. What we're going to do endangers everybody's livelihood, and the courts don't like that, Taylor. You don't think you're just going to get up from the table and march to the cage with a million or more dollars in chips? They're going to review the tapes before they pay, and anything suspect, any meaningful glance, any fucking thing whatsoever is going to make them review them again, and if they look long enough, they may find an angle where they can see what I'm doing. And if they see that, you and I won't be sharing a million dollars. What we'll get is arrested and led off the floor in handcuffs."

"I'm getting your point," Taylor said.

"Neither one of us needs to be distracted by him or wondering what he is or isn't showing on his face. We need to be thinking about the signals between us. *Only* the signals between us, and we'll work them out so they can't see them. And there can be no words at all. Nothing that isn't normal dealer/player jive."

"Have you talked to anybody in Vegas yet?"

"Yes, and it's as good as I had hoped. A job at the Mirage. I start in a couple of weeks. I'll probably need a week or so to get my bearings and make sure I'm on a high limit table. We're looking at a little less than a month from tonight."

Taylor turned on his computer and saw a "YOU HAVE MAIL!" message blinking. He opened it:

From: <honkeytonkwoman@aol.com
To: TRobFaulk@memphis.edu>
Sent: Friday, June 25, 11:23 PM
Subject: No Subject

Hey there. Here's your message. Tell me more about the Bahamas. I don't know what else to say. Bye, Stormy.

He hit "REPLY."

From: TRobFaulk@memphis.edu>
To: <honkeytonkwoman@aol.com
Sent: Friday, June 25, 11:24 PM
Subject: The Bahamas

Hey back at you. It looks like we'll be heading your way in a few weeks. I intend to play for a few days and then you and I will go down to St. Thomas and burn 'em up. I'm going to have a stake, sweetie, enough for us to stay as long as we want. Sand and sun and a whole lot of what Vegas doesn't have, beautiful girl: water. The ocean lapping at our toes. Rum punches and cool breezes. Get your shades ready. Oh, and your bikini. Definitely your bikini.

I'll keep in touch with you this way and with postcards if I can't get to a computer. And the telephone, of course. Check your e-mail occasionally, and I'll let you know what's going on. Right now, just keep the last couple of weeks of July free, and after that . . .

I think about you all the time. Please tell me why you told the Reverend what you did . . . do you still want to be with him?

Taylor pushed the "SEND" button and navigated onto the Internet.

WELCOME TO STARGATE, THE BEST THING ON THE INTERNET

Connect TRob Faulk

CONNECTED

Page Soothsayer=Are you here?

Soothsayer pages=Always, apparently.

Page Soothsayer=Can I come to you?

Soothsayer pages=Why not? I'm bored tonight.

TEL Soothsayer

You find yourself in a desert at midnight. The stars are bright above, and the moon shines brightly, illuminating ominous forms of huge saguaro cacti. For a moment you think you are alone, but then you perceive a young girl walking toward you out of the darkness . . .

Trob says=Hanging out in the desert, yet. I never know where I'll find you."

Soothsayer says=I like it out here. Have you ever been to a desert in the west?"

Trob says=Not really. Driven through it a few times on the way to Vegas, but I never paid much attention. I'm about to, though. I'm going out west on a little sightseeing expedition. Mix pleasure with business."

Soothsayer says=Is that right? And I wonder what kind of business are you doing there?"

Trob says=Blackjack.

Soothsayer says=And you're going to ask me for a prediction . . . which I've already given you if you got the message I left for you the other night.

Trob says=So the hard luck thing was a blanket prediction, huh? Well, guess what, little lady. I don't need luck."

Soothsayer says=Oh really? How so?

Trob says=Let's just put it this way: I know I am going to win.

Soothsayer says=So says every stupid gambler.

Trob says=I have a reason for saying it.

Soothsayer says=What would that be?

Trob says=Let's talk about something else. Hey! Let's talk about your orgasms. Or the presence of God as manifested by absurdly ill-fated or unlikely coincidences.

Soothsayer says=Those subjects don't, like, grab me. Maybe the coincidence thing is worth talking about . . .

Trob says=Yes, I want to tell you a story, something that happened to a friend of mine. Play with yourself while I type this . . .

Soothsayer says=Waiting.

Trob says=Playing?

Soothsayer says=Waiting.

Trob says=This friend of mine told me about a strange thing that happened to him when he was younger and hanging around in the bars. He and his roommate walked into a little cafe one night and there was a biker there, name of Kenny Campbell. Now, I happened to have known that particular louse: a character who came from an old and so-called "good" family who was so violent that he'd been fired as a bouncer, yet, from a couple of the meanest bars in Memphis. A little too enthusiastic about his job, you understand.

Next thing you know, my friend's roommate is into it with the guy. Ken Campbell hit him with a pipe and knocked his front teeth out. After the hospital and all that shit, they (my friend, hereafter known as "Plaintiff's Corroborator," and his roommate, hereafter known as "Plaintiff") decided to take it to court. And they did. Plaintiff's Corroborator testified that Campbell had started an unprovoked fight resulting in an injury that would plague Plaintiff for the rest of his life. When the testimony was over, Plaintiff and Plaintiff's Corroborator were appalled to observe that the judge did next to nothing to Kenny Campbell. Gave him probation and a fine. A slap on the wrist.

Plaintiff's corroborator put it to your reporter, my sweet, like this: "We knew we were in for it. We knew he would come back. And there was nothing to do but wait. Both of us slept with pistols. We talked it over and decided that, of the two weapons we had, I would keep the Luger, he the .22, since we figured he would go for my roommate first. I would have the better shot and so should have the bigger gun. I lay awake night after night praying that I wouldn't have to kill a man.

"One day I was at work when I got a call. Kenny Campbell had just been shot six times, killed while breaking down someone's door to get at him. The man's roommate had shot him. With a Luger."

What do you make of that, seeress?

Soothsayer says=What?

Trob says=What do you mean, what?

Soothsayer says=I missed that.

Trob says=I TYPED ALL THAT AND YOU "MISSED" IT?

Soothsayer says=Sorry. I was playing with myself.

Trob says=SHIT! Oh well, first things first, I guess. Put your feet up on my shoulders while you do that."

Soothsayer leans back and puts her feet on Trob's shoulders, tickling his ears with her toes . . .

Trob says=Heh heh . . . this is a pleasant sight. Ahem, you wouldn't do anything like you did the other day, would you?

Soothsayer says=Tell me about the situation with your wife . . . it turns me on.

Trob says=There is no situation with my wife. The divorce is going through.

Soothsayer says=And the situation with your girlfriend?

Trob says=We'll be together for a while. Up to a certain, very important point when I come into a lot of money.

Soothsayer writhes and bucks, locking her ankles around your neck.

Soothsayer says=Tell me more.

Trob says=Well, the young woman I've mentioned is in the picture . . . I'll be in her league after that certain, very important point."

Soothsayer says=And then you're going to dump your girlfriend . . . the succubus, you call her."

Trob says=Well, I wouldn't put it quite that callously. Let's just say that my options will be open.

Soothsayer pulls her sweater above her breasts and moans.

Soothsayer says=Slap my breasts.

Trob slaps your breasts, firmly but gently. But not too gently.

Soothsayer says=Keep talking. Tell me your lousy plans. Show me what a no-good-bastard you are. Make me one of your bitches.

Trob says=You're really into this, aren't you?

Soothsayer says=Be rough with me.

Trob grabs you around the waist and jerks you toward him . . .

Soothsayer moans and says=Keep talking . . . tell me how you're going to two-time your bitch girlfriend . . .

Trob pulls you closer, says, "Here's something you're going to like . . ."

Soothsayer smiles at you with her half-closed eyes, says, "Wait, my darling.

There's something I must do . . ."

Trob says=Uh oh . . . what?

Soothsayer says=There's somewhere I must go . . . can you guess where?"

Trob says=NO! NO! Not the bathroom!

Soothsayer smiles coyly and says, "Uh huh."

Trob says=Lil—Soothsayer, for God's sake!

Soothsayer gets up and walks toward the bathroom. For a while there is running water, and then you hear the sound of the window raising. Then there is silence, and after a few minutes you wonder what has happened to her, walk to the bathroom and open the door. She is gone. There is a note on the back of the toilet.

Page Soothsayer=Why did I expect anything else? Where are you?

Page Trob=Where you can't find me. Did you read the note?

Page Soothsayer=Let me guess: does it have something to do with luck?

Page Trob=You got it, or rather . . . you won't have it.

Page Soothsayer=I won't need luck, naysayer.

That player is ignoring you.

Page Soothsayer=I won't need luck, naysaying cockteasing window-hopping harlot.

That player has disconnected.

Disconnect

Trob disconnects

Taylor told the Reverend of the impending trip. "Vegas and no Stormy to distract us," the Reverend said. "Maybe we'll do better together this time." Ramona gave notice at Southern Belle, and was told that her services were no longer required, effective immediately. The three of them met at Taylor's apartment to make plans. They had some time to kill before Ramona started at the Mirage, and Taylor had cash, a lot of it. He looked around at his apartment, thought of leaving it, and suddenly a weight seemed to fall off his shoulders. "Hell, let's go the day after tomorrow," Taylor said. "We'll do some sightseeing and take our time getting there. I've always wanted to tour the west instead of just seeing what was outside of a casino door." He paused for a second. "Ramona, what about your car? Should we take it and let me sell the truck tomorrow?"

"My car's leased through a deal with Southern Belle. I'll have to turn it in . . . but what about the lease on my apartment?—yours, for that matter."

"Fuck a lease," the Reverend said. Ramona glared at him. He was just the kind of guy to say that sort of thing. But he had a point. She would never be back and no one had any obligations. It was time to go.

A couple of days later, at ten o'clock in the morning, they pulled out of Memphis with luggage stuffed in the bed of the truck under a tied-down sheet, and crossed the Mississippi bridge into the delicate green of the Arkansas rice farms. An hour or so later the delta gave way to the rocky foothills of the Ozarks, and the straight highway began to wind a bit. They had a late lunch from a cold buffet in Little Rock, the apple cobbler stale and rank, in a home-cooking place whose sole appeal was that it was open. Within sight of the courthouse, this part of downtown in the pre-Clinton presidential years seemed nearly abandoned.

Back on the highway they saw dead armadillos lying beside the road raising jagged claws to the serene and indifferent sky, and the remnants of truck-tire blowouts which resembled the armadillos from a distance. They arrived in Dallas before nightfall and found the Kennedy assassination sight, surprising to Taylor because the street Kennedy's motorcade had followed turned directly beneath the window from where Oswald had shot and the angle was more acute than Taylor had imagined. At one point, Oswald might have shot straight down on Kennedy's head from the fourth floor of the warehouse, which really wasn't that high. Something about the Zapruder film had always made the shots seem longer than they were . . . Taylor wondered why Oswald hadn't shot when Kennedy was approaching, why he had waited until Kennedy was past him, pulling away. Possibly he had hesitated; more likely he thought that a receding target would make it harder to identify where the shots were coming from.

They walked along the famed grassy knoll, sat down beneath a memorial and watched the setting sun turn the marble walls purple and crimson. The Reverend was engaging some other tourists in conversation about conspiracy theories and wandered away, leaving Taylor and Ramona alone. He looked at the purple light softening her profile and highlighting fine blond hairs along her cheek as she looked toward the window from which Oswald had fired, and something in him almost swelled, something that had nothing to do with money. Then she turned toward him, and her gaze was hard for a moment before her expression flickered and softened. But the hardness lingered in his mind. "Where were you when Kennedy was killed?" he asked.

"I don't remember," she said.

Taylor looked at her in disbelief. She was essentially his age. One of the most vivid memories of his childhood was that of his entire school assembling and kneeling in prayer at the first mention of the news, even before Kennedy was pronounced dead. Everybody remembered that day. This was yet another of Ramona's oddities that showed him how little he knew about her.

Well, there was no point in pursuing it. They got up and found the Reverend. After a western barbecue at a nearby restaurant recommended by one of the women the Reverend had befriended—beef, not pork, which the Reverend insisted was not barbecue at all—they drove into the Texas night watching the exit signs appear and disappear with the same rhythm of flaring brightness fading into darkness that the lightning bugs striking the windshield shared, the ephemera of travel . . . Eastland, Cisco, Baird, and somewhere outside of Abilene stopped at a decrepit motel and, with a nerve-jangling buzzer on the office door, woke up the house-robed and disheveled proprietress. She opened the door, rubbed her eyes and further smudged her mascara, then gave them a key to a seventeen-dollar room.

It had been a long day and they turned in almost immediately, with Ramona barely having time to complain about Taylor's choice of lodgings. While the Reverend snored raucously in one bed, Taylor and Ramona slept chastely in the other. Taylor felt the warmth of Ramona's body across the space that separated them. It was warm enough, he supposed, but it did not burn.

They left Abilene on a luminous morning, the sky so blue it hurt their eyes, and caught their first glimpse of the giant shadows of clouds moving across the plains and a road as straight as a gunshot cleaving the distant hills. It was beginning to look like the Reverend had no intention of relinquishing the front passenger seat to the lady, and simply commandeered it himself by jumping in first, *sans* discussion. Ramona sat in the back, and occasionally Taylor caught her angry eyes in the rear view mirror. She emanated hatred that Taylor could feel all over him, like wet wool, but to which the Reverend seemed oblivious. Taylor was a bit amazed at both of their capacities for sustaining ill-will; he would have had to do *something* to diffuse the vibes in the car before he could ride in it.

Still, it was their problem, not his, and he breathed in the smells of summer meadows, butterweed and purple clover, and listened to the steady hum of the straight-eight engine guzzling gas—they were getting only about 200 miles per tank—until they stopped for lunch in Odessa. Other than a few futile "look at that's" on Taylor's part, they had driven in silence for hours.

They walked into a Mexican restaurant and the eyes of three waiters sitting at a bar raised expressionlessly toward them in the darkness of the building. Taylor looked at vinyl-padded walls, molded plastic bas-relief sculptures of Spanish armor and swords, a black velvet bull frozen in death throes with particolored pikes decorating his back and flanks—something to stimulate an appetite—and a smell of mildew and grease.

They had a quiet meal, although Taylor did manage to generate a subdued and pragmatic conversation about their travel plans; Ramona wanted to stay in fancy hotels (after all, she and Taylor knew that they had plenty of money and would soon have more); the Reverend wanted to camp out, believing that one couldn't experience the west any other way. His idea of the west was that of cowboys and gunfighters; like many felons, he saw himself as a kind of Jesse James, an outlaw rather than a petty criminal. Taylor, since his gambling had begun, had developed a profound proclivity for being penny-wise and pound foolish. He never bought his cigarettes without money-off coupons, never dipped into his gambling stake to buy, say, clothes (or a car, for that matter), and would worry more about the gas it took to get to Tunica than the five hundred dollars he lost when he got there. They hashed out a kind of compromise and then they were on the road again, dipping toward New Mexico and Carlsbad Caverns, where Taylor wanted to see the bats.

They arrived in Carlsbad with an hour to spare before the bats emerged. Deciding to tour the cave, they entered a giant maw somehow obscene and emitting a reek of guano as swallows wheeled like seabirds in the cathedral-sized opening. Following lighted trails down a pathway hewn in rock, Taylor turned and saw the opening behind them disappear. Suddenly he was aware of the darkness and the tons of rock overhead, and was surprised to find himself claustrophobic. He fought not to grip Ramona's arm too tightly.

The Reverend, on the other hand, seemed unfazed. "This would have been a hell of a hideout in western days," he said. No doubt. Within the intricacies of the cave, a person could get lost forever. The only way out of the absolute darkness would be to follow the sound of a bat's wings. Early in the century, the cavern had been mined for guano which, a brochure informed them, had been forty feet deep, The bats roosted in an area that was at present off-limits to the public. This was just as well, Taylor thought. They had lived here for more than thirty thousand years and if not isolated and protected would quickly have been killed, he imagined, simply for someone's pleasure in killing them.

They took an elevator down to the deepest level open to the public, and there the trail led them past a stalactite as big as a train lying across the floor of a dim and echoing room . . . they kept their voices low, fearing reverberations. The stalactite had fallen twenty thousand years ago, the guide said. Taylor looked above him. There was no reason one of the others might not fall now. Suddenly, his fear threatened to turn into panic. He could see himself buried here, lost forever beneath the rocks and dirt. "Let's get out of here," he said, and when the other two heard his tone of voice they started for the elevator. He felt some relief as they got back on the elevator and started climbing, but did not entirely relax until he had walked out of the cave into the light.

They sat in a concrete amphitheater surrounding the opening as a park ranger lectured. They were informed that they would soon see Mexican free-tailed bats, relatively small bats that migrated somewhere in Mexico in season to an unknown roosting place—Carlsbad Caverns was discovered by someone following bats but no one had as yet found the counterpart cave in Mexico—and returned to Carlsbad each year to their dank and pitch-black home in the bowels of the earth where they hung upside down from the cave roof and had contact with the sun and its energy only insofar as did the flying insects they consumed. "Here they come," the guide said, turning around toward the opening, and Taylor, Ramona, and the Reverend craned their heads as if they might miss something. "No, sorry," the guide said, turning back. "I just caught a group of swallows from the corner of my eye." The swallows fell ominously silent. "*Here* they come!" the guide called.

Suddenly he was obscured in black wings. A massive cyclone of bats began billowing like smoke from the cave, each individual making a counter-clockwise circle as it came out, then spiraling into the sky where the plume they collectively formed began to break into numberless winged points like a negative of the evening sky which would soon be reversed as the stars winked into visibility and the bats winked out. There were thousands, millions of bats, and the guide could be seen only intermittently as the solid stream fluctuated into turbulence like blown smoke, then re-formed as before. The bats were like cards streaming from a shoe, each individual bat a card, the solid body they formed the game in its entirety.

Taylor noted that there was a periodicity in this sudden appearance of form out of chaos. At varying intervals, the cyclone of bats dissolved into shapelessness, then reappeared. In a sense, what he was observing was entirely random, because the perceived form was a projection of his own mind: why was the cyclonic form any more meaningful than the "amorphous" cloud? In any case, the intermittent perception of a pattern was itself problematic because there was no way to predict when it would appear; one could only predict from observation that it *would*. And how long must the pattern last before the mind perceived it? The bats formed a pattern that was both random and not-random. It was as though, somewhere in that turbulence, there was an underlying order causing it: an algorithm of chaos.

Taylor looked at Ramona and the Reverend, who sat with their mouths open. "Reverend," Taylor said, "how many seconds before the park ranger is visible again?" They played this game as darkness fell and the bats continued to fly from the cave in a ceaseless stream. Thirty minutes. Forty five. The bats were still coming out when they got up to leave.

"Well, that was worth seeing," the Reverend said.

"If you like bats," Ramona observed.

It was the Reverend's choice of lodgings on this night. They camped out in the park beneath a mountain; after a quick trip to town, Taylor cooked hamburgers on one of the communal grills, and then they stretched three hammocks between gnarled Mesquite trees. The Van Gogh stars spread like a parody of themselves across the sky as Taylor rocked himself into a dreamless sleep. At the first glimmer of dawn he awoke and saw an unfamiliar animal, something possum-like but far too quick, eating a crust of hamburger bun from a nearby picnic table. As Taylor raised his head, the animal was gone in a flash. He rolled out of the hammock and hung a percolator from crossed sticks above a campfire, and coffee was ready when Ramona and the Reverend stirred. Bird calls, silver light, summer smells from the dewy grass, the scent of coffee, and they were on the road again.

From Carlsbad they drove toward Tucson, stopping only to relieve themselves along the side of the road, dipped south and spent the afternoon in Tombstone at the Reverend's insistence. Taylor had been enjoying the scenery from the car and could have kept driving; however, walking among the graves in Boot Hill Cemetery, he enjoyed the epitaphs. They were nearly all obviously modern lamentations written for tourists but clever nonetheless: "Here lies Les Moore/Four Slugs from a .44/No Less, No More." Nice, but Taylor preferred the laconic ones: "Hattie Johnson: Poisoned" . . . "Arlan McDougal: Hanged by Mistake." Ramona was bored but the Reverend seemed to have found his element, insisting that they tour an old whorehouse called the Birdcage Theatre and eat a steak at a cafe on the Main Street. A thunderstorm blew up and they lingered over dessert while the Reverend scanned the street outside, saying "Man, I was born a hundred years too late." The thought of the Reverend making his own law with the .38 he was carrying right now beneath his shirt was a frightening one. When the rain stopped, he bought a rattlesnake belt at a gift shop. Whether or not it was Ramona's turn to choose, both she and Taylor were exhausted, and he sprang for a kitschy room that would have cost twelve dollars in Memphis but was $112 in Tombstone.

The next morning Taylor rousted everybody out of town, stopping at a convenience store for donuts and coffee. Then they made a brief stop at the Saguaro National Forest, where they observed giant green cacti of surprisingly little interest to Taylor, who supposed he had seen them too often in movies. The Reverend hammed it up for a few snapshots, grabbing his ass and looking askance at the spikes. Then through Tucson to spend a night in Phoenix with a friend of Taylor's.

Michael Hunter was a computer expert and occasional player whom Taylor had met at the first casino in Tunica, *Splash*, a tent on the Mississippi River that netted about 150 million in its first year of operation. It stayed open for another couple of years before competition forced it out of business and the backers walked away with two or three hundred million. Well, some businesses fail.

One day Taylor was playing at Splash when he noticed another card counter at the table. Most people wonder how anyone can tell that a player is counting. It's a simple matter of someone being able to count the cards and watching another player's bets. While the casino has a lot of people to watch, good players at the same table nearly always recognize each other very quickly, and after the man's bets mirrored Taylor's for a few hands, Taylor caught his eye. Michael smiled. When Taylor was comped for lunch, he asked for two passes, and invited Michael to go with him.

They became friends and played together for a while as Taylor worked out the rudiments of "pushing the dealer." A large bettor at the first position works with a smaller-betting compatriot at the last position who "saves" a bust card for the dealer, standing on such hands as ace-six when the next card is likely to be a ten—the strategy Taylor later adopted with the Reverend. Too often, though, Taylor found that Mike didn't feel like making the drive down to Tunica. He didn't play as much as Taylor wanted to, perhaps because he made enough money at his job writing software for FedEx, but more likely because he just wasn't a gambler. It was an experiment, a hobby, to him. His wife didn't like it, and when she started objecting to the time he was spending at the casino he stopped.

Mike was out as far as being a prospective partner. Soon after he got a job in Phoenix working for Motorola on the cellular phone project known as Iridium—telephone signals bouncing off satellites from any point to any point, so that someone could be in the Amazon jungle and hook up to the Internet—and moved. Taylor had stayed in touch over the telephone, but had not seen him in a couple of years. When he realized he was coming out west, he called. Mike had invited the three of them to stay over for a few days if they wanted.

Taylor negotiated the directions to a development in Scottsdale, then found the address. They parked in front of the house and Taylor couldn't help being aware that his truck looked conspicuous in the neighborhood. The Reverend affected a studied casualness, but Ramona seemed taken aback. "So this is the way computer experts with real jobs live," she said. From behind a ranch-style palace, the edge of an Olympic-sized swimming pool glittered.

They piled out of the truck and walked toward the house. At the first knock Mike opened the door with a smile on his face while his wife peered over his shoulder, looking friendly but dubious. Melinda obviously had resolved to make the best of itinerant gamblers in the house.

Taylor made the introductions and soon enough, after being shown their rooms and changing into "bathing suits"—Ramona actually had one; Taylor and the Reverend had shorts—they were eating a southwestern style dinner that Melinda graciously prepared and served in the backyard beside the pool. Then they lounged around in the lingering heat of the evening, vibrant on Taylor's skin like menthol. He watched Ramona dive in and swim from one side to another in the blue pool. Nothing gleamed.

Michael had computers all over the house. In fact, there was a laptop out here that Ramona had been fiddling with. Taylor had wanted to hook up to the Internet, a concept that still seemed impossible to him if the computer wasn't plugged into a wall, and while Michael was ready to show him how, Ramona couldn't be bothered. She was in the middle of an important game of solitaire. "Not now," she said, in an ugly tone of voice, and Taylor knew not to push it. Her manner had been piqued and distant since they arrived, almost rude, and Taylor had been struggling not to be embarrassed. The rest of them talked . . . of the game, of course, until Taylor sensed Melinda's discomfort, and then of the Iridium project, which Mike said was doomed to fail not because the concept was faulty or that technological expertise was lacking, but because of bureaucratic mismanagement within the company. Someone would make it work. While Taylor was attentive and even half-interested, his mind was on something else. He wanted to get to one of the computers inside, someplace private.

Ramona seemed as content as she was likely to be, playing on the laptop or now and then jumping into the pool. The Reverend was lying in a lounge chair with a beer and a cigar. Taylor told Mike that he was going inside to close his eyes for just a few minutes. Once inside, he hurried down a hall and looked into the bedroom where he had seen Mike carry his and Ramona's bags. On the desk, there was a computer. Taylor felt his heart start to pound just a bit. All of this was puerile and adolescent, no doubt, but was sex not most interesting in adolescence?

WELCOME TO STARGATE, THE BEST THING ON THE INTERNET

Connect TRob Faulk

CONNECTED

Page Soothsayer=Are you here?

That player is not connected.

Page Soothsayer=Please be here.

That player is not connected.

Page Starguide=Please, ma'am, leave a message for Soothsayer. Please tell her that I miss her. Also, please let me know if she comes on line. I need her to spin her fantasies for me. Or are they my fantasies?

Starguide pages=Done, Trob. There is a message for you from Soothsayer.

Page Starguide=Please send it to me, mistress.

Starguide pages=The following message was left for you by Soothsayer.

I'm hot and you haven't no idea how much I want you. I was laid down on my bed reading my stupid school book when I thought of you coming in. I would look up as you walked in the room. I would pull the blankets off my legs. You stand there watching, our eyes never coming unglued.

Then you would sit next to me on the bed. Kiss me hard and harder. My back would ark up to you. Then you would raised up a little and I would start to unbutton your shirt. You would undo the buttons of my silk nightshirt that feels cool.

I would moan a little more, needing you. Want you. Then I would pull you up to kiss our lips, our tongue in knots in each others mouth! You pull my arms over my head as you started to bone me, harder and faster!! Now is the time for you to see my tattoo. You turn me over, wanting doggy style. There it is! On my butt, a little background of a twenty-one table, an ace of spades and a down card an inch or so below it. You ask me is it a blackjack. I say you tell me. You say "Mmmm, on a purple chip." When it was over, you would hold me tight and say you love me. And I would say I love you to. And then we would sleep tangled up all night in each others arms and legs and stuff.

Nothing would make me happier.

Starguide pages=Trob, Soothsayer has just arrived. She is in the park.
Page Starguide=Yes! Thank you, mistress.
TEL Soothsayer
Trob has entered the park. There are children playing near a pond. A young girl is sitting beneath a willow tree.
Trob says=My love, I got your message.
Soothsayer says=So now you know how I feel.
Trob says=That was so sweet. The exclamation points were a stroke of genius. I used to get letters from a girlfriend in high school that did that. The content, of course, was not exactly the same.
Soothsayer says=You liked the exclamation points? They just came naturally.
Trob says=Well, of course . . . like the content?
Soothsayer blushes=Um, yeah.
Trob says=Also, I love the tattoo. And it's definitely a blackjack. Hey! Can you tell where I am?
Soothsayer says=You're very close to me.
Trob says=RL, my sweet.
Soothsayer says=RL, indeed. Yawn. Aren't you in Memphis?
Trob says=No, no. Already on my way to Vegas. I'm in Phoenix.
Soothsayer says: So far away . . . and what exactly are your plans in Vegas? How are you certain you're going to win?
Trob says=You know the dealer you met? Wait! I mean the dealer I told

you about . . . the one that's my girlfriend?

Soothsayer says=Of course. Your stupid affair.

Trob says=She's a very talented woman.

Soothsayer says=You've got the nerve to tell me that after the message I left for you?

Trob says=No, no, my love. She's talented with her hands . . . no, no, I mean she's talented with her hands when it comes to cards.

Soothsayer says=Oh . . . and?

Trob says=And I'm going to win a lot of money. A lot. And then do you know what I'm going to do?

Soothsayer says=Tell me.

Trob says=I'm going to take the money and leave for the Bahamas with another woman. The other one I was telling you about.

Soothsayer says=Say that again.

Trob says=I'm going to leave with the money and another woman. Heh heh.

Trob says=Are you lagging?

Trob says=ARE YOU LAGGING?

That player is ignoring you.

Trob says=No, no, wait!

Trob pages Soothsayer=Please come back. I need to tell you more.

Soothsayer has disconnected.

Page Starguide=Mistress, I have a message for Soothsayer. Tell her that she didn't let me finish. I was just having fun pretending to be worse than I am . . . like she does. Tell her that I intend to split the money with the dealer, that I'm leaving with the other one, yes, but that I'm going to give the dealer half of a lot of money—a LOT of money—tell Soothsayer that will considerably ease the pain of my desertion. Tell her that I will get in touch with her from the Bahamas when I find a computer . . . I'll buy a laptop . . . tell her that I know who she is—oh, hell, I know it's you,

Lillian—and that I think this game we've been playing has been, is, more erotic than . . . well, RL. And thank you for having a tattoo designed in my honor.
Starguide pages=Got it, Trob.
Disconnect

Taylor sat there looking at the machine. There was something exciting about Lillian pretending to be eighteen, something self-effacing and submissive. And the tattoo and the exchange surrounding it . . . she must have gone to the trouble to research a bit. Lillian wasn't a gambler; she wouldn't have known a purple chip was worth five hundred dollars. She still didn't know that the down card would have been beneath the ace vertically, not horizontally, that the only way to represent a dealer's blackjack hand would have been to show some of the down card fanned out from under the ace rather than lying beneath it with a space between the cards—and had probably put it there because of the association with "down." He wondered whether or not he should have told Starguide to tell her he knew who she was, because things would change when she knew he knew. The fact that it had been unspoken had been a large part of the game, a large part of the eroticism. Both of them knew the other one knew, but if they weren't sure . . . or pretended to be unsure. . . well, it was done now. A message to the Starguide couldn't be retrieved. No matter, Taylor thought. He had come to admire Lillian so much that she need only pretend to be herself.

He lay down on the bed and fell into a dreamless sleep. It seemed like hours later when Ramona came in, told him to take his shoes off and move over.

The next morning they had breakfast and a swim before leaving. Mike had already left for work and Melinda directed them to a fancy mall she thought they might like to see. The only one interested was Ramona, and Taylor was happy to drive there because she wanted to see it. All morning she had been putting out seething vibes that embarrassed him in front of Melinda and made him grateful Mike was gone. PMS? When she was like this she was scary, and Taylor would have taken her anywhere.

They walked through misters placed along the outside walkways, something Taylor did, in fact, find interesting. The air was so dry that one walked through a fine water spray and was dry again in a moment. In the humid south, one would have stayed damp all day and probably mildewed before drying.

The next stop was Sedona, with its tourism-driven claims as some kind of spiritual vortex. Taylor couldn't get out of an astronomically-priced giftshop with paintings of Indians and eagles fast enough, nor did he feel particularly spiritual when he was forced by the Reverend to park the truck and stand on a mystical rock, where the Reverend snapped his picture and asked whether or not he felt the confluence of psychic vibrations.

Taylor insisted they go on to Flagstaff. The truck labored and threatened to overheat as they climbed into the mountains, but the needle on the heat gauge stayed just below the red and at last they labored into a high campground. Ramona had about had it with camping but the truck too had about had it, and Taylor insisted that they give it a rest, regardless of her attitude or the fact that he could immediately tell that the air was too thin for him. Both he and the Reverend, heavy smokers, were beset with altitude sickness. Moving slowly, attempting to ignore their headaches, gasping for breath, they spent the afternoon getting ready for the night by hanging the hammocks and putting together a fire in a tactical spot, which later had to be moved and rebuilt when it threatened to set Ramona's hair ablaze. That night, Taylor would find that he was too cold to sleep and that it did not get any easier to breath even if he lay motionless after piling on blankets and dirty laundry trying to stay warm. Ramona, a nonsmoker, was cold but okay. Taylor and the Reverend spent a miserable, sleepless night fighting for breath.

The next morning they left hurriedly without breakfast, heading for the Grand Canyon. A couple of hours later they pulled the truck over at an overlook and Taylor felt for the first time that something in the west had lived up to its reputation—or surpassed it. This was something alien. He had never seen so much space on dry ground. The Canyon was an otherworldly expanse more unbelievable in its breadth than depth, dotted with tabletop mesas varicolored and immensely unreachable. He instantly understood why the area had not been developed with condos and theme parks: it was simply too rugged to *be* developed. From the rim where they stood, three or four mesas beyond, he saw tiny white mountain goats the size of lice climbing a sheer wall.

After looking for half an hour, they drove deeper into the park, found some facilities, and attempted to bathe with coin-operated showers that cut off without so much as a warning buzz while soap was still in Taylor's hair, and nobody had any more quarters. Everyone, even Taylor, decided it was a good idea to get a room at the Grand Canyon Lodge. They slept for most of the day, then went down to dinner at sunset. Set on the rim, this hideously expensive hotel in a so-called high rustic style had a view of the canyon out of the dining room windows. They were served a meal that cost Taylor a small fortune—the least expensive thing on the menu was a fifteen-dollar hamburger—and as they lingered over after-dinner brandies and peach ice-cream, the sunset turned the hard rocks and sharp edges of the canyon ice-cream colors as far as they could see. Taylor kept wondering what it would have been like to be an early explorer and to see this, to wander to the edge of the Canyon without having the remotest idea of what was about to reveal itself.

They stayed three days as Taylor tried to placate Ramona, who had hardly smiled or had a word to say since Phoenix, and then dipped south again, bypassing Las Vegas because they were too early. Ramona's job didn't start for more than a week, and there was no point hanging around together in the town. There was always the chance that someone would put Ramona and Taylor together. They plotted a great circle around Vegas.

From the Canyon, they traveled south, and in Williams, Arizona, picked up Route 66 heading into California. This once-famous highway had suffered considerably more than Highway 61. In the fifties, it had been the most traveled road in America—at least the part close to Los Angeles. Here, as they drove through the desert, the road was abandoned. Even ghost towns were rare: now and then, in the sweltering heat, they listened to the truck tires hissing through the remains of a ramshackle town with the paintless doors of derelict cafes hanging open and rusting railroad cars lying on their sides like dead animals beside the road. Then heat and sand. Ramona began to express certain misgivings: "Why are we on this road? If anything goes wrong with this rattletrap, we're going to be in deep shit."

In a place the map called the Music Mountains they stopped on the side of the road to relieve themselves. Here, other than the road, there was no sign of human beings at all. The wind played ominously through the mountaintops like a low organ note, hence the name, Taylor supposed. The Reverend didn't get out, saying that he was dehydrated anyway, Ramona squatted behind a yucca plant, and Taylor stood beside the car, looking around and listening. A sense of foreboding came over him and he had to make a conscious effort to pull himself together. This was a place for bad luck.

Back in the truck no one said a word but merely stared ahead as they picked up speed. Taylor kept hoping the tension between the Reverend and Ramona would let up, especially since some of what was coming from Ramona seemed to be aimed his way, presumably for bringing the Reverend along. He had told her the situation and he was beginning to get tired of her attitude.

Just off the road there were yucca plants and small cacti dotting the desert. In the middle ground, as far as one could see until mountains interrupted vision—and there were *always* mountain ranges on the horizon—there was only a near-featureless expanse as the green faded into empty stretches of sand, the monotony broken only by the stately procession of the huge shadow of a cloud moving as slowly and inexorably as a clock as it crawled up and over the side of a mountain range, and in the far distance those mountains were arranged like studies in perspective, generally three deep, the nearest a malevolent gunmetal grey gleaming in the sun, the farthest always a soft shimmering blue.

Now and then a dirt road overgrown with cacti, as if it had not been used in a very long time, snaked off the highway. These roads never seemed to go anywhere discernible. They merely went toward the mountains until they become ribbons, then threads, then disappeared. Roads to oblivion.

They drove all day, got lost, somehow found themselves heading into Death Valley in the afternoon, changed course, and drove into the night. Taylor could find nowhere to stop, and in any case, he had seen a sign pointing to Yosemite, a place he had always wanted to see. This was an agreeable destination for everyone, and as the moon rose the mood inside the truck finally mellowed just enough for the Reverend to wax philosophical: "This is a night to consider the miracles of God."

Ramona snorted. Taylor, hoping to keep things pleasant, said quickly, "So tell us, Reverend." They leaned into sensuous curves as the road began to twist through hills. Ponderosa Pines raced down the hillsides to stand at attention beside the truck as it sped past. The night air was scented with resin. Possibly even Ramona would relax under the full moon silvering the pines.

"I'll tell you later. Maybe I'll write a sermon. For the moment, consider just the miracle of adaptation we're about to see, the giant sequoias." Having never finished high school and, in fact, barely begun it, the Reverend had, like many self-educated men, a particular pedantic tone when he was elucidating something. "They grow only here and in one small spot nearer San Francisco. This is the only place on earth where the conditions are right for them. Probably, there were also giant trees eons ago which have become extinct. God writes drafts, then revises. Knowing which drafts will persist or be repeated, and how often, is the challenge, as we know from the blackjack tables. Actually, that's all God writes, drafts. Some of what we see looks like the final form, but that's because we won't live long enough to see the end. Those stars above us, for instance, may already have ceased to exist."

They entered Yosemite at the high meadows and Ramona looked up at the stars spread like silent fireworks across the sky. Taylor didn't put it beyond her to be cynical about stars but she was quiet.

"Yeah," Taylor said, "I think all we have to do to see the redwoods is turn toward a place called Tuolumne Grove." Not wanting to interrupt the Reverend's train of thought, he added: "Well, sometimes I do think I've seen evidence of God in this or that adaptation. I guess the detractors of Mr. Darwin would find that ironic. Anyway, certain miraculous creatures and peculiar symbioses seem beyond coincidence. I remember seeing in *National Geographic* a praying mantis of pink and purple that waits, perfectly disguised, only on a pink and purple orchid in Borneo. Then there's the ghost bird of Haiti, the only pollinator of a certain species of night-blooming moonflower."

"The ghost bird of Haiti?" Ramona asked.

"In Haiti there's a rare hummingbird that roosts in caves during the day, like the bats at Carlsbad. It flies at night, feeds only on this particular flower. Over the ages the bird has lost pigmentation, like the 'glass' fish one finds in cave ponds. Its feathers generally appear white with a certain translucence, like watery milk, but in a certain slant of moonlight the feathers and flesh are transparent, and the bird looks like a flying skeleton. If that bird didn't exist, the flowers would die out because they couldn't reproduce, and if the flowers didn't exist, the birds would become extinct, since those flowers are its only food."

"And that bird is made of the same molecules that make dirt," the Reverend pontificated. "The laws of physics don't contradict life, but they can't account for it either."

At that moment Taylor turned around a bend in the road and immediately came to a complete stop. Standing in the middle of the road staring into the truck lights, with its tongue hanging out of the side of its mouth, was a wolf, supposedly long extinct in Yosemite.

"I don't believe it," Taylor said.

"It's a sign," the Reverend said. "Life is so incredibly unlikely I'm just surprised it isn't a unicorn."

The wolf looked at them with its yellow eyes for a long moment, showing neither fear nor surprise. It was one of those encounters with a wild animal where the humans are wide-eyed while the animal itself seems unperturbed. It turned its head slowly away, then ambled across the road and began to trot casually into the meadow. Soon it was out of sight. As he peered after it, Taylor spotted a small wooden sign on the side of the road and drove closer. "Tuolemne Grove," it read, and an arrow pointed at a narrow lane winding down from the high plains.

Taylor turned down the lane and into darkness as the stars thinned, then winked out above them. The moonlight dimmed and sputtered like a candle, then it too was gone. In darkness approaching that of Carlsbad, they were suddenly aware of huge shapes around them, and just as suddenly Taylor was spooked. They were in a grove of redwoods, and they were bigger than Taylor could have imagined. In some sense, they weren't like trees at all. They were like huge, silent buildings. When the road leveled out, Taylor stopped the truck and turned it off. The three of them got out slowly. Sometimes, as it has been said, silence can be like thunder. It filled the grove. No one said a word for a long time.

"The unicorn is less unlikely," Taylor finally said in a whisper.

"And what makes us *decide* to stay here in the darkness and take this in?" the Reverend asked.

"Stupidity," Ramona said. "We don't know what kind of animals or serial killers are lurking around this place. Let's get out of here."

Her tone was insistent but Taylor wouldn't have needed much convincing. There was something eerie about being down here in the darkness with these shadowy giants hovering over them. They piled back in the truck, drove out of the grove and halfway across Yosemite along the winding road that began to seem remorseless as Taylor tried to pick up speed and find a place to spend the night. They discovered at midnight that Yosemite lodge was full, then drove all the way through the park and out the other side where, exhausted, they rented a teepee for fifty dollars from an enterprising young man and lay down in their clothes on a blanket thrown on the ground inside. Sleep was not long in coming.

In the morning they cleaned up at a stream behind the teepee which the proprietor pointed out with one hand while rolling a joint with the other. At Ramona's insistence, they then drove back into the park to Yosemite Lodge for breakfast. If Taylor had thought the Grand Canyon Lodge was expensive, this place clarified the concept. Three dollars for a small glass of orange juice, ten dollars for a couple of eggs. Had Taylor not been flush with cash, he would have glanced at the menu and left.

There was the same explanation that they had heard at the Grand Canyon (Taylor wasn't above asking the white-shirted, haughty waitress even if Ramona did glance sidelong with embarrassment): transportation fees. No doubt it was difficult to get food delivered here, but they were not on the moon. The three of them had a perfectly normal breakfast which they might have had at any pancake shop that cost Taylor eighty-five dollars with the tip, and when he paid he felt his face flush, whether with anger or humiliation at being such a sucker he was not sure.

From Yosemite they drove to Lake Tahoe, which is divided by the state line between California and Nevada, and noted the distinction. On the California side there were upscale shops not unlike those on Rodeo Drive in Los Angeles, while on the Nevada side casinos blazed with neon. Taylor felt a familiar tug . . . but why should he gamble? A good gambler always took the sure thing. It was just a matter of time.

From Tahoe they drove toward Reno, then stopped at Carson City when no one but the Reverend, who was ready to play, could see any reason to be there. Taylor decided to drive across the desert to a little town called Ely, which he had been through years before. They could play there. Population about ten or twenty thousand, he couldn't remember. A small town. Two or three casinos, a couple of whorehouses. An old train from the turn of the century, the "ghost train of Ely," that chugged tourists around abandoned mines and local points of interest, like the "gentlemen's ranches" which the conductor-guide took pains to point out were legal businesses. Ely was very different from Vegas in that it was a small town, had a small town ambience, and was therefore much stranger, really, more distinct in its old west ethos.

As they turned out of Carson City they saw a sign: *Highway 50, the Loneliest Highway in America*—probably a justifiable billing. There wasn't a gas station or a building of any kind for fifty miles, and what little commerce they saw along the entire stretch, probably one hundred and fifty miles, amounted to an old-fashioned filling station here and there, operated for the most part by leathery-looking middle-aged women who wound up in this scorched terrain at the ends of the earth for reasons known only to them. In the main, what they saw was the road, cutting straight as a pistol shot as far as the eye could see, and the ever-present mountains looming on the horizon. Taylor let the truck, which did have a powerful engine in reasonably good shape, fly on this road, and soon enough they were hissing along at over 100 miles per hour.

Taylor began to take note of the same kind of side roads he had seen snaking off Route 66: dirt roads that led to the distant mountains for no apparent reason. What could there possibly be up there that would make someone build a road to it? Finally, curiosity got the best of him. He jammed on the brakes, turned, and fishtailed onto one of the roads to nowhere.

"Where are you going?" Ramona yelled.

"I'm going to see where this road goes."

"Can't you see it goes into those mountains on the horizon?"

"Yeah, so what? What's in those mountains?"

While Ramona and the Reverend howled objections and Ramona actually tried to grab the steering wheel, Taylor drove over sparse cacti and dusty weeds. Ramona finally calmed down when she realized he had no intention of changing his mind, and after forty-five minutes the mountains began to fill up the windshield. Then the road skirted some boulders and traveled parallel to the mountains until they actually circled the range and were riding on the far side. Soon enough they were climbing, winding up the side of the mountain, with all three of them eyeing the truck's temperature gauge. As they gained altitude and looked across the desert, no sign of human beings was visible other than the dirt road stretching ahead and behind.

The road leveled off at a small plateau or mesa, and Taylor turned around a rocky bend. They entered a ghost town. "Good God," the Reverend whispered. It was either an old west town or something relatively recent built in the same style. They had entered on the main street, and on both sides derelict paintless buildings, some of them with their doors leaning open, stretched for two or three blocks—they could see dirt crossroads—and Taylor pulled the truck to the horse rail running the length of the street and stopped.

All three got out of the truck wordlessly. Silence stretched into the immensity of the sky, then was broken when a hand-painted hotel sign above the street creaked in a stir of hot wind. Taylor and Ramona mounted some steps to the wooden walkway alongside the shop entrances and began walking, peering inside the shops as they passed. The Reverend crossed the street and walked parallel to them, his shoes scraping on the walkway. Taylor gazed into a doorway beneath the sign: "Apothecary." On the far wall, he could see dark glass bottles aligned on sagging shelves.

They pushed the door open and entered. A floor of wide pine planks creaked beneath their feet. Dust motes raised by their steps sparkled and swirled in a shaft of sunlight. Breathing in the smell of sun-scorched wood and the desert itself, Taylor turned and saw the clear imprint of their steps in the dust. They moved toward the back shelves—the bottles all seemed to be empty—and glanced into a darker room at the rear of the store, where a three-legged chair leaned toward an open window. "I wonder how many years it's been waiting here," Taylor whispered.

"Waiting and watching out that window," Ramona said softly, then laughed. "Why are we whispering?"

"Is there anybody here?" Taylor called, raising his voice. Then, gaining courage, he walked to the door and yelled at the top of his lungs: "Is there anyone in this town?" He waited, listening, then laughed and turned back to Ramona.

They were looking at each other when a gunshot broke the silence. Neither broke the gaze; their eyes simply widened as each attempted to see an explanation in the other's eyes. Then another shot stirred them into action, and they hurried toward the front door, peering out cautiously.

The Reverend was trotting down the street holding his .38 with both hands in front of him, practically on top of a huge rattlesnake which was frantically trying to escape. The Reverend kept blasting a few feet in front of him and missing, but at last seemed to graze the snake, because it suddenly stopped and drew itself into a defensive posture with its head high and its tail rattling. The Reverend kneeled on a level with the snake, aimed carefully from two feet away, and blew its head off. The body leaped and curled around itself in a lascivious embrace with death.

When the snake shuddered into stillness, Taylor and Ramona walked into the street. The shots, seemingly echoing from the rocks, were still ringing in Taylor's ears. The Reverend picked the snake up by the tail and shook it out like a line. It was about six feet long and astonishingly thick in the middle. Reaching down tentatively, Taylor found that he could not get his hand around it. Despite the fact that he had often seen caged rattlesnakes, Taylor felt like he was seeing one for the first time. It seemed exotic, a rare and fabulous creature: a Haitian ghost bird, a narwal, a unicorn. This animal, however, emanated menace rather than good fortune, even in death.

Suddenly Ramona was squatting beside him, running her hand down the length of the body. "It's beautiful," she said. "Look at the diamonds."

"You're not afraid of snakes?" he said.

"Not dead ones," she said.

"Where did you run into this thing, Reverend?" Taylor asked.

"I opened the door to the hardware store around the corner and it was curled up in the middle of the floor, rattling at me. I took a shot at it and it crawled right past me out the door and into the street." He paused. "We'd better be careful. If anybody gets bitten out here, we're in for it. It's a long way to any help."

Taylor began mentally framing his argument against Ramona, who would surely start asking to leave. He had already made up his mind he wanted to spend the night here. But Ramona said nothing.

"You're right about that," Taylor said. "Where's your other gun?"

"The .22?"

"Whatever."

"It's in my bag in the truck."

Taylor walked to the truck and dug around in the brown paper bag the Reverend used for luggage. He fished out a long-barrelled Colt revolver and a holster. Walking back, he strapped on the holster and put the gun in it.

"There," the Reverend said. "Now you look the part. Has anybody seen anything with a date on it? What the hell are we dealing with here?"

"We haven't seen anything yet," Taylor said. "But let's keep looking. For all we know, this is a nineteenth-century town. It looks practically archaeological, that's for sure. Hell, the doorknobs and the fixtures are probably worth a fortune as antiques. There are chairs and bottles, God knows what else."

"Let's go check out the hotel," the Reverend said. "Maybe there's a guestbook or something with a date in there."

They approached the hotel, pushed open the door, and walked into the lobby carefully, scanning the floor for snakes. A couple of stuffed couches with horsehair coming out of them sat on the dusty floor. In front of them, there was a large counter or built-in desk. Behind that, a U-shaped stairway led to a second story of rooms, straight above and behind the desk. Taylor walked around the desk, looking for papers. There was nothing, just empty pigeonholes.

"Do you notice that smell?" Ramona asked.

"Yeah," Taylor said. "It's all over town. Everything smells scorched. Too many years in the desert sun."

"I wonder if there are still beds in those rooms," Ramona said. She began walking up the warped stairs carefully, making sure they would bear her weight. Taylor and the Reverend watched as she began opening doors on the first level. "This one's got a dresser, but no bed," she said.

"Nice view of the desert out the window." She climbed to the top level, opened some doors, and then leaned out over the balcony stair rail. "Hey, guys," she said. "This room is still furnished. Sheets and blankets on the bed, yet. I guess they didn't want to carry anything down from up here when they left."

"Whoever *they* were," Taylor said.

Taylor and the Reverend started upstairs. Standing in front of an open bedroom at the top, wearing shorts and a tight t-shirt, Ramona looked for a moment like a woman waiting to do business, and the thought occurred to Taylor that this place might not have been entirely a hotel. Ramona waved them into the room, and Taylor and the Reverend looked at a museum scene or a set out of a western movie, complete with a pottery wash basin on a pine stand beside a tiny bed. Taylor looked out the window, and saw the desert through dry-rotted white curtains, then back at the room. "How can this be?" he asked.

"What do you mean?" Ramona said.

"I mean, I think this town is more than a hundred years old. I don't see anything in it that isn't antique . . . nothing modern. But there was a road that led here—a *dirt* road, yeah, but why hasn't someone scavenged everything?"

"Maybe because there's no one here, no one even close," the Reverend said.

"We can't be the first people to find this place since it was abandoned. That's impossible. It's only an hour off the highway."

"But who in their right mind would turn on that road?" Ramona asked, squinting her eyes at Taylor.

"Again," Taylor said. "The *road*. It was built to come here. It was built to come here from the highway."

"So how old is the highway?" Ramona asked.

"Probably sometime in the fifties is my guess," Taylor said.

"Well, maybe scavengers took the things they valued and left behind what was old junk to them," Ramona said.

"That *could* be," Taylor said.

"On the other hand," the Reverend said, "this stuff isn't necessarily old. The furniture and the architecture are just crude. If the three of us were going to build some chairs or a house right now, this is what it would look like. This town is home-made."

"Everything we've seen so far, anyway," Taylor said. "Let's keep looking."

Ramona led the way as they started looking into the other rooms. She was at the far end of the hall when she opened a door and Taylor heard her gasp. "Jesus!" she cried, jumping back out of the doorway, and as Taylor and the Reverend watched, edged back into it, then called out, "Holy shit, this is creepy."

"What?" Taylor and the Reverend both said, approaching cautiously.

"Take a look," she said.

They peered into the doorway. Like the other, it was a completely furnished room. In the bed, with covers up to its neck, lay a crude female mannequin with a blond wig askew on its head. Taylor went into the room, peered down at the mannequin, and pulled the blanket back. Part of the blanket crumbled in his hand, and through a cloud of swirling dust he saw that the figure was dressed in a flannel nightgown and had formed a deep impression in the mattress.

"Is this somebody's idea of a joke?" he asked. "They put a mannequin in the bed to scare the shit out of somebody like us?"

The three of them looked around in the room, trying to find something that would fix the place in time, if nothing else. They could not find anything at all. No papers in the dresser drawers, nothing in the bottom of the crudely nailed pine armoire that was completely free of decoration and looked as if it had been hammered together by a semiskilled carpenter.

The mannequin itself was wooden, and the wig was actually yarn of some kind, more like a doll's hair than an attempt at realism. Perplexed, they looked at each other in silence, until the Reverend said, "Most of these abandoned towns were mining operations. Let's see if there's a mine out there, just out of town."

The three of them were soon walking through the town, which did not take long. The whole town was precisely nine blocks, three by three. It was bound on two sides by granite cliffs rising sharply upward, so that two streets butted into rock (one of them *through* the rock, because it was the road they had driven in on) not twenty yards beyond the last buildings. On the third side, an abrupt precipice dropped off into the desert, but on the fourth, facing due west, the plateau on which the town stood sloped gently down. This entire side was open to the desert, and this was the prospect the hotel overlooked. The three of them trotted down the sandy slope and looked around, to the limits of vision, then back at the town. All of the buildings leaned away from them, as if in time they would lie down.

"All right," the Reverend said, "Now let's skirt around the edges. You two go that way. I'll go the other way. We'll walk all the way around this town, and if you see a mine, yell."

Taylor and Ramona started walking. Almost as soon as they began to walk along the granite rock face behind the town, they saw it: at a break in the rocks where softer dirt formed a steep hillside was the entrance of a mine shaft. They ran toward it and started in, then both of them stopped short.

"My God," Taylor said.

"Here we go again," Ramona said.

At the far end of the shallow shaft, which extended into the hillside only about twenty feet, a figure sat motionlessly against the back wall.

"Let's hope it's a mannequin," Ramona said.

The shaft did not extend into the hillside far enough to be completely dark. Taylor approached the form in dim light. "Yeah," he said, "it's another mannequin. Call the Reverend, tell him we found the mine."

While he heard Ramona yell and the Reverend answer from the other side of the town, Taylor looked at the dusty mannequin. This one was male, its canvas pants and shirt dry rotting at the knees and elbows. It was propped against the wall like a rag doll, its legs straight out in front. Taylor walked out of the mine shaft and saw the Reverend coming.

"Well, here it is," Taylor said. "This is why the people were here. But I'd appreciate it if you could explain these mannequins to me."

The Reverend peered around one of the posts at the opening, then walked inside and looked around. He walked to the far wall, paying little attention to the mannequin, just looking at the sides and the top of the shaft. Then he came out.

"OK," the Reverend said pensively, "you got a little town here that might be thirty or forty years old, might be a hundred or more. Either way, what's it doing here? Out here in the middle of nowhere where there can't possibly have been any business and there's no mining going on."

"What do you mean, no mining?" Taylor said. "What did you just come out of?"

"I'll explain it to you at the service tonight."

"Huh?" Ramona said.

Taylor was preoccupied, thinking aloud: " A little mine . . . maybe some religious group looking for isolation," he said. "Maybe shelter from Doomsday."

"Could be," Ramona said. "Except for one thing: where's their fucking church?"

"I've been wondering exactly that," Taylor said. He paused, then continued: "It might have been one of those sects that didn't believe in churches. They could have used the hotel lobby, or even the hardware store, for assemblies. Or maybe they were running around naked out here in the desert without any meeting place at all, praising God and foaming at the mouth."

"You two can stop that kind of talk," the Reverend said. "I've been missing a religious service. In point of fact, I'll lead one tonight. I'll expect you to be present here at a few minutes before sunset for an informal service and prayer."

"Tonight, Reverend?" Taylor said.

"Give us a break, please," Ramona said.

The Reverend pulled the .38 out of his pocket and discharged it into the air. "Silence!" he screamed, while the shot was still resonating across the desert. "Service at sunset." He looked at them until he was certain he had their complete accord, then stalked up the slope toward the town. At the top he turned and called down to them, "After services there will be canned Spam and crackers, which I had the foresight to buy yesterday. There are also soft drinks in my bag in the truck. You're welcome to drinks now, but save some for later." He walked out of sight.

"You know he's stark raving insane, don't you?" Ramona said.

"Be that as it may, I don't suppose a prayer or two will hurt us," Taylor said. "Anyway, I suspect we're going to have to earn our dinner. He's got the food."

"I would insist on being taken away from this place, but you and I need to spend some time alone tonight."

Taylor grinned. Ramona looked at him with a blank expression and said, "No, not that. We need to rehearse the game."

"Yes, of course," Taylor said. "Hmmm . . . maybe that too?"

"We'll see," Ramona said. "Let's go get one of those drinks."

They began to walk up the slope. Taylor again noticed that all the buildings were leaning slightly away from them, as if they would someday fall backwards to the rocks and the desert floor. He considered this was perhaps a clear indication of the town's age for someone with the right kind of training. "I wonder how long it takes for buildings to begin to lean like that in a place where's there's hardly any wind or weather," he said. "If we were archaeologists, maybe we'd know."

"But we're not archaeologists," Ramona said. "We're players."

"And under the right circumstances, " Taylor said archly, "we're thieves."

Ramona visibly winced at this and walked in silence for a moment, then turned toward him: "Is that how you think about this? Let me tell you something"—Taylor was stunned at her tone of voice; it was the strongest emotion he had ever seen her show—"I've been in this dirty business all my life. I've seen people lose their houses, their jobs, their families, and their lives. I personally have dealt to two people who tapped out, went out in the parking lot, and shot themselves in the head. God knows how many others killed themselves that I'm not aware of. I've seen the bosses chuckle about a suicide and say, 'The stupid son-of-a-bitch shouldn't play if he can't afford to lose.' I've seen the wrong people win and the right people lose. I'm simply doing what I can to rectify that. You think of yourself as a thief if you want to. As far as I'm concerned, I'm a champion of justice."

He looked at her expression. "Sorry, Mona. I was just making a joke. Yeah, that's us: champions of justice."

They walked to the truck and dug cold strawberry soft drinks out of the Reverend's cooler. The drink went down a bit like sand as Taylor, perplexed at the depth of Ramona's reaction, continued to appraise her and hope she would lighten up. The last thing in the world he needed was for her to get angry with him.

At sunset they walked down to the bottom of the slope overlooking the desert and found that the Reverend had culled from somewhere two

decrepit chairs and set them up facing a lectern fashioned from wooden boxes. Dutifully taking their seats, although the man himself was nowhere to be seen, they shielded their eyes from the setting sun and saw that the desert was smoldering with pale fire, a muted blaze of pastels ranging from lilac to purple. "So this is why they call it the Painted Desert," Ramona said. Taylor nodded wordlessly.

The Reverend appeared at the top of the hill and walked processionally down the slope, wearing his collar, tattered vestments, and a godly expression. He walked past them, stood behind the lectern, and cleared his throat. "My children, we pause at the hour of vespers to acknowledge our Creator. Let us pray . . ." Taylor bowed his head while Ramona continued to scan the colors of the desert.

"Our father in heaven, we are sojourners toward Vegas, where we pray you will deliver us from sixteens against tens, twelves against deuces, and sucker low-count splits that play into the dealer's hands. We pray for the power to differentiate hope from cold expectation, and the wisdom to know when expectation is failing. If the cards are aberrant, we pray they be aberrant in our favor, dear God, for we would rather be lucky than good. More than anything, we ask that you grant us that rarest of occasions at the table when the count and the cards coincide exactly, and we feel as if we are looking down into a stream that a moment ago was opaque but now, because of the angle of light, is visible to the bottom and we see the smallest pebble, the shifting grains of sand. We ask for the slightest intimation of the algorithm at the heart of chaos, the merest glimpse of you, our god. This is what we pray. Amen."

Taylor muttered an amen, Ramona smirked, and both gazed up at the Reverend. He was standing directly between them and the setting sun, so that he was haloed with light. "Very impressive," Taylor whispered.

"My reprobates," the Reverend intoned, "this evening I will speak to you of certain improbabilities, and to suggest that the lack of appreciation of God which you two show is, in fact, a failure of the intellect. Therefore, tonight I will deliver *The Sermon of the Three Miracles.*"

"Please, no miracles," Ramona said.

"Be quiet," the Reverend said, and there was something in his tone of voice that made it clear that he wasn't in the mood for sarcasm from the congregation. "Neither of you would know a miracle if it hit you in the face, which it does every day."

He glanced over his shoulder. "The sun that is setting behind me, for instance, depends for its existence on a precise balance between the nuclear fire at its core and the gravity that contains that fire. Were the fire any greater, the sun would have long ago exploded into space. Were the gravity any stronger, it would have collapsed into itself and we would not be here to ponder it, for it is not only the sun, our star, that sustains us, it is of starlight that we are made."

"I like that, Reverend," Taylor said. "That's good. 'Of starlight we are made.'"

The Reverend pulled a couple of pieces of paper out of his back pocket, unfolded them on the lectern and began to read. "We may consider the world first," the Reverend said. "Why is there a universe, my children? Why this particular universe anyway?" the Reverend glanced up, frowned, and plowed on, undeterred by Ramona's yawning.

"Why this elaborate system?—which we should understand from jump street argues against the universe being infinitely old. If that were the case the tendency of things to run down would long ago have won out, disorder taken over order, loss of energy maximized itself. In short, the stars would have burned out."

"I like that. The 'in short,'" Ramona said.

The Reverend ignored her. "So consider the beginning, since there has to have been one. Consider one of the paradoxes of creation: the fact that time itself is a part of physics, and if the universe began, or was caused, then our notion of cause and effect is turned upside down, because causation happens in sequence, in time. If God created time at the moment he created the universe, then we are left with the impossibility of God existing before there was a before."

"Let's not go into that," Ramona said.

Taylor registered the man of the cloth's expression and understood that this wasn't the least part of a joke to him. "Are we allowed to ask questions, Reverend?" Taylor asked.

"If your questions are to the point," the Reverend replied.

"OK, granted that the universe had a beginning, why should we necessarily think that a god created it?"

Ramona groaned, sensing a theological debate coming on.

"We shouldn't necessarily think anything," the Reverend said. "We're modern men, after all. We derive our beliefs from the evidence. I'm simply asking you to consider the evidence."

"Okay," Taylor said. "If the universe had always been here, it wouldn't be here." He was silent for a while, trying to gather his thoughts and at the same time stop Ramona from doing something he had not seen since he spent one nightmare semester teaching high school. "And everything physical depends on something else, something outside of itself for explanation. A ball rolls; it was pushed. The earth forms; gravity pulls space dust together. But if the physical thing in question is the entire universe, there is nothing outside of it, by definition, to cause it."

"Nothing but God," the Reverend said. "The universe in which we live, and which you take for granted, is the first miracle."

Ramona stretched lavishly, arching her back and showing off her breasts, which were really not bad, not bad at all. The Reverend glared at her. "You haven't even grasped the strangeness of this town. How could you begin to appreciate the strangeness of the universe?"

"What do you mean?" Ramona said.

"I'll explain after the sermon," the Reverend said.

"On to the second miracle," Taylor said.

"Life," the Reverend said. "A living organism is made from the same atoms that make up a rock, basically. An atom of carbon inside a living organism is no different from one in a pencil, so life is not reducible to some magic formula of ingredients. I don't doubt that you're alive, but I couldn't say the same thing about an atom taken from you. So how can something living be built from dead materials? In point of fact, there's no quantifiable difference between a live human being and a dead one, except that the latter's dead."

"Well, that is a difference, Reverend. What's the third?"

"Consciousness," the Reverend said. "Our perception of these shapes, this life, this universe. What's the difference between mind and brain?"

Ramona continued to squirm and spread her legs like a naughty high school girl trying to distract the teacher.

The Reverend continued to ignore her. "As I was saying the other night in the redwood grove, we might suppose that this weird town in which we find ourselves has a predictable effect, and that we would respond in a predictable way. However, just as was the case in the redwoods, we have something outside both the hardware and the software, as if were, which allows us to *decide* how to respond."

The sun was going down and the Reverend concluded, "The act of observation causes a change in the nature of a subatomic particle, causes it to become, as it were, either here at one place and motionless or at an indeterminate place and moving, like an ace somewhere in the deck. If it's been played, we know where it is. If it hasn't, we don't. In the act of knowing one aspect, we exclude the possibility of knowing the other. Neither the atom nor the ace makes the choice. We do. When the ace appears, we agree that it is 'there.' If it doesn't appear, it is *somewhere else*. We have to observe its presence or its absence before one or the other is 'real.' This is exactly why a player sometimes has the eerie feeling that he is 'thinking' the dealer's perfect hits into existence, by fearing them, or that he *knows* when he is going to win.

"Thus we start from the constituent parts, as infinitely small as the universe is large, or as unknowable as the random order of the cards until they've been seen, and conclude that consciousness brings the universe into existence. End of sermon, end of service."

"Bravo," Taylor said.

"Thank God," Ramona said reverently. "Now, what about this town?"

"In a moment. Now that the service is over, I invite the flock to fellowship in the form of a bottle of bourbon I have stashed right here." He pulled out a bottle from beneath his vestments. The three drank a toast to the universe with gulps of bourbon the Reverend poured into paper cups.

"Was this an all-purpose service tonight, Reverend, or did it lean toward any particular denomination?" Taylor asked, mainly for Ramona's benefit. She was the only person Taylor had ever met who had never been taken to church as a child.

The Reverend thought for a moment. "I would have to say, due to the cerebral nature of the sermon and the fact that the pastor fully intends to get drunk as a lord, that it was decidedly Episcopal."

"What are you celebrating, Reverend?" Taylor asked.

"I'm not celebrating anything. This place gives me the creeps, and if we're going to spend the night here, I'm going to sleep drunk and dreamless."

"The place is a little strange, sure," Taylor said, "but it's beautiful here. Quiet and peaceful. I've got a feeling I'm going to sleep very well, thank you."

"A little strange? There are two very important things, missing things, that you two rocket scientists haven't noticed."

Both Taylor and Ramona listened attentively. "What's that?" Taylor asked.

"You've been all over the town. Hasn't it occurred to you that something very necessary simply isn't here?"

"For God's sake, Reverend, what are you talking about?"

"Water. A well, you morons, a well. There's no water here."

"What?" Taylor said. "How did they drink?"

"Your guess is as good as mine. Obviously, they brought water from somewhere else. Now the question is not only why this town was here with no apparent means of support—I'll explain, I'll explain—but why it existed, period, without water."

"It did have a means of support," Ramona said. "The mine."

The Reverend rolled his eyes and looked toward Taylor, as if he too couldn't be that stupid. When it looked as if he could be, the Reverend continued: "That's not a mine, morons. It's not even a mine shaft. It's just the beginnings, just a start into the hill. Nobody came here for that, because nothing was coming out of it, and they didn't come here and build an entire town on speculation either. First you get a producing mine, then you get a town. You don't get a town and then half a mine shaft."

"Then it's just a movie set," Ramona said.

Taylor knew this wasn't the case. "No," he said, "I've been an extra on a couple of movies. This place is both too complete in some ways and not complete enough in others. I mean, what's the purpose of so many rooms that duplicate each other when any single one of them would do? And on the second point, I'll give the Reverend credit for noticing what you and I should have seen, Mona. When I was an extra in a crowd scene set in the fifties, everyone was required to take off their wristwatches except me, because mine was an antique. The camera was way up there on a boom, and in the movie all of us in the crowd were barely visible, let alone our watches. With that kind of attention to detail, which was common to both films I worked on, why would they not have built a fake well here at the very least?"

The three of them remained silent, pondering this, as the tip of the sun slipped below the horizon. No one had an explanation. Nevertheless, Taylor considered that there was after all no reason to be afraid of an empty town. There wasn't any point in hitting the road now, at sunset, and driving for God knows how long through the desert before arriving at a hotel when they already had one here for free. Most importantly, Ramona was due in Vegas tomorrow evening. Driving time was down time, and this was the last night for them to rehearse the game. For that, they needed privacy: it was not something they could do in front of the Reverend.

Taylor had another sip of bourbon and asked Ramona to go the car and bring back a soft drink to mix it with. She hesitated. She wasn't the kind of woman to do errands, but when she saw the look in his eyes she studied him for a moment and then started up the slope. When she was out of earshot, Taylor spoke to the Reverend: "Listen, Reverend. Ramona and I need some time alone tonight, if you get my drift. We're going to take a couple of the camping lanterns up to the first room at the hotel. Because it's so quiet here, I'd appreciate it if you would stay out of the hotel, at least for a couple of hours."

"No problem. Hell, there was a decent cot in a back room at the hardware store. I'll pull it out into the street, away from the snakes, put a sleeping bag on it and sleep out there."

"You don't have to do that. Just come on in the hotel later tonight."

"No, seriously, I'd just as soon stay out of these buildings. I don't know why, but I would."

"Suit yourself, but thanks for letting me have the time."

Ramona came back with a soft drink in one hand and a lantern in the other. They mixed up a couple of drinks for themselves while the Reverend declined, saying he preferred to drink straight. They left him sitting in the desert in the gathering darkness, swigging from the bottle, and carried their drinks up the slope.

Inside the hotel, they put the lantern in the center of a table in the lobby and Taylor found a chair. Ramona remained standing on the other side of the table, as she would be in the casino, and pulled a deck of cards from her purse.

"All right," she said, "the first and foremost thing you need to understand is that every move, every glance we make that night, will be on videotape. The tape will be reviewed before they pay you the kind of money you're going to win. And if there is anything whatsoever that can be interpreted as a signal, or a pattern, they will review it again. These people are smart, Taylor, smarter than you think, and if we're not real careful both of us will be led out of there in handcuffs rather than you going to the cashier's cage with a million dollars worth of chips."

Taylor nodded silently.

"Now, obviously you can't win every hand. Even if that was a good idea, it would be impossible, because I can't know every card I'm dealing. Depending on how closely they're watching me—and we can be damn sure they'll be watching close once you start winning—there'll be times when I can only know the first card. More often than not, in fact. It won't be like that day in the hotel, when I could do practically anything in front of you and you wouldn't notice because you don't know what to look for. They know. Now, watch."

She shuffled the cards, offered him a cut, and said, "I know the first two cards and the card on the bottom. But they aren't good cards. There's a seven and a ten on top and a deuce is on the bottom. In this situation, you may lose through bad luck. I can give you seventeen against a deuce, but I won't be able to know what I have down. Or I can give you twelve against the seven, a probable loser. Or you can have nine against a ten, which also might lose. Now, this is important, and it's something I don't think you understand. I know these three cards, but once we use them up, I can't know what another card is until I get a peek at the deck while I'm gathering up the discards from that hand. Then, I'll only be able to see the top card and maybe, maybe, the bottom one. If it's an ace, I'll signal you to bet big, but I won't know for sure that I'm not going to put a five on that ace instead of a ten.

"If I'm dealing the first hand of the deck I'm probably going to know three cards. If one of them is an ace and one is a ten, it's a no-brainer, of course. If there is an ace, nine, and seven, I can give you twenty, but I won't know what's under that seven I give myself, or what I'm going to hit it with. You follow me? I don't know whether or not I'm going to turn over a four and then hit the eleven with a ten and beat you. So, in that case, I will have signaled that you should bet the maximum but I'll win the hand. Taylor, this *will* happen occasionally. Don't let it throw you. Just hang in there. I can't beat you like that in the long run, that's for sure.

"There may be times when I withhold the ace that I know is the first card. Why waste it on, say, nineteen or even twenty when I can give you a blackjack a hand or two later? In that case I might signal that you should bet the maximum and beat you on the hand before the blackjack, so that it doesn't look suspicious when you always raise your bet at just the right time."

"So what are the signals?" Taylor asked.

"I'll show you in a minute. The important thing is that they vary. That way the surveillance people can't establish a pattern because there won't be one. Now, hopefully we'll be playing one on one, you and me. I should be dealing at a hundred dollar minimum table, which ought to keep the fleas from jumping in and out, but if there is another player at the table that will complicate things. But this is what we'll do head up.

"First, stop counting the cards. It's not necessary in this situation, and your mind must be clear to concentrate on this. If it is an odd-numbered deck, the first, third, and so on, my thumb will be on the left side of the deck, my left, your right, if it's a winner. If it's a loser, it will be on the right side of the deck. If I don't know, it will be in the middle of the deck. The opposite will be true on even numbered decks. Thumb on the right, it's a winner."

"OK, and you'll only know one way or the other after I make the cut, right?"

"Right."

"So I can't place my bet on the first hand until you have the cards right in front of me, ready to deal."

"Yes, but that's not really a problem unless you start making it a problem, always putting out a small bet out and then raising it the moment before I deal. It's better to have no bet at all, and then act as if you're communing with the stars, trying to make up your mind."

"OK, let's try it."

She shuffled the cards and held the cut card out to him. He inserted the cut card, she reversed the stacks, and held the cards up to deal. Her thumb was to her right, his left.

"I bet a hundred," he said.

She dealt him seven/three against a nine. It was easy enough to see that she had given him the best hand she could with the three cards at her disposal. Obviously, he was going to hit; the question was whether or not he should double his bet.

"Are we going to work out hits the same way?" he asked.

"Yes, they will be the same signal as the hand they come on."

Her thumb was directly in the middle of the cards.

"So you don't know what's coming?"

"No, I dealt the three cards I knew."

"OK, just a hit." He scratched for a hit and a ten fell in front of him. She turned over nineteen. "Why didn't you double?" she said, smiling cynically.

"Hindsight is 20-20," he said.

She picked up the discards and turned toward him. Her thumb was on the left of the cards.

"I bet five thousand," Taylor said.

An ace appeared in front of him, but it was followed by a seven. Eighteen. She showed a six up. Again, it was a question of whether or not to double. He looked at the cards in her hand. Her thumb was in the middle. She didn't know. He waved it off. She turned over a ten for sixteen and hit with a three which gave her nineteen and would have given Taylor twenty one on the double. "A case in point," Ramona said. "Shit happens."

She gathered up the discards and turned to deal. Her thumb was on the left. "I bet five thousand," Taylor said. He looked down at twenty, two red kings glowing in the soft lantern light. Ramona showed a three, turned over a ten, and hit with an eight, which she threw down disgustedly on the table. "Shit happens again! Sometimes you just can't beat these cards."

When she turned to deal her thumb was again on the left, all the way to the left. But the last couple of hands had left Taylor feeling skittish. "I bet a thousand," he said. A blackjack appeared before him.

"You can't lose heart," Ramona said. "If I say you're going to win, you're going to win. It's just a matter of time. There will be surprises, sure, but they won't last."

She reshuffled the cards. This was an even numbered deck, the second. After the cut, she held the cards, ready to deal. Her thumb was on the right. "I bet five thousand," Taylor said. He got sixteen against a ten and looked at the cards in her hand. Her thumb was on the left. A bad card. He waved off what he would normally hit. Ramona turned over a five for fifteen and busted.

"That time I had three cards that I knew I could bust with. I just gave you a random hand."

"Ramona, there's one problem, a major problem. What if I get confused about whether we're playing an odd or even numbered deck? Then I'm gonna be misreading the signals."

"That's why you need to practice *not* counting, keeping it out of your mind, so you don't lose track. But if you do it isn't a big deal. Just ask me how many decks you've played, as if you're trying to tally up how much you're winning a deck. If I say, 'Oh, I think that's about fifteen,' you know that the next one is even, and the thumb on the right means a good hand."

"But that won't work after I've been playing for hours. You can't say something like 'Oh, that's about one hundred and seventeen decks.'"

"No, but *you* can. You can say out loud, 'I've played through about 100 decks, it seems like.' That way I know that the next one is 101, and it's odd. Thumb on the left. Needless to say, it's best to keep up with it, but if it seems like we're getting out of synch, it's a simple thing to verify it."

Like a slap, there was a shot outside and crashing glass, then the Reverend's voice in a drunken cowboy yodel. Taylor walked to the door and called out, "Reverend, what are you doing?"

"It's Saturday night and I'm shooting up this one-horse town," he called. But he hardly needed to raise his voice, which carried from the far side of town in the stillness. In a lower tone that was as clear to Taylor as if he had been standing beside him, the Reverend said, "Fill your hand, you sniveling egg-sucking snake." There was another shot and the sound of a window breaking.

"Ahem, Reverend, who are you shooting at?"

"I'm shooting at a lilly-livered sodbuster who's trying to ambush an honest gunfighter." A loud explosion . . . this time the shot was closer. He had come to the next street over. Taylor could hear his footsteps.

"Hey, Reverend, you know not to shoot toward the hotel, don't you?"

Ramona had come out in the street. "Stop that shooting, you fool!"

she shouted. Suddenly the Reverend appeared at the far end of the street and turned toward them, his arms hanging at his sides, a dim figure silhouetted in moonlight. "Fool?" he said softly. "Fool?"

"Take it easy, now," Taylor said. He had heard something in the Reverend's voice. Ramona had heard it too, and Taylor could feel her poised for flight. He was suddenly aware that he was still wearing the holstered gun. Fighting an urge to drop his hand toward it, he kept his arms crossed over his chest and repeated, "Take it easy, Reverend."

From the end of the street the Reverend's voice came out emotionless and flat. He was intoning the last rites.

"Stop it, Reverend," Taylor said, staying perfectly still.

"Draw, you yellow-bellied coward," the Reverend said, low and cold. They stared at each other and the Reverend raised his gun slowly. Taylor watched his hand, saw the .38 buck, and heard a bullet hiss past about a foot over his head before the shot boomed. Ramona screamed, "Stop it! Stop it!" Now she was angrier than she was afraid. She stepped in front of Taylor and screamed, "You're drunk. Stop this bullshit!"

The Reverend stared at them for a long moment. "You need to grow some cojones, professor," he said. "Hiding behind a woman's skirt." He turned and slowly walked the cross street until he was out of sight. Then there were three quick shots and Taylor and Ramona heard windows blowing out.

"That fucking maniac," Ramona whispered.

They went back into the hotel and leaned a chair beneath the front door knob, since the door itself did not have a lock. "He's drunk and crazy," Taylor said. "Let's go up to one of the rooms in case he does start shooting in this direction."

Upstairs, Ramona said, "You see why I didn't want to bring him now, I suppose."

"He's just playing . . . at least I think he's just playing."

"It's a hell of a joke. He's dangerous, Taylor."

Sporadic shots continued outside, then finally stopped. Taylor went downstairs and peered out the window. The Reverend was laid out flat in the street in front of the hotel, the proposed cot forgotten, the gun and the empty bottle fallen in the dust beside him. Taylor went back upstairs and told Ramona that it was all right now. She took a deep breath. "I hate that bastard."

"I know," Taylor said. "Now, where were we?"

"Here," she said, and began dealing cards out on the bed. "I imagine we're safe as long as he's passed out."

They played into the night, Taylor voicing his imaginary bets. He lost twenty thousand dollars out of the first two decks. After an hour, he was up only fifty thousand. After two hours, he had it: a million. There it was.

Taylor lay back on the bed and stretched, reached for Ramona's hands and pulled her down beside him. They had not made love since the trip began.

"Taylor," she said, "I'm exhausted."

He was not to be put off. It was important that they do this. It would cement something. Ramona lay still as he took her clothes off. In the act itself she seemed mechanical, as distant as a prostitute. Once, Taylor lifted his head from the pillow and caught her gaze. She seemed far away, this woman who loved him enough to share a million dollars with him. No doubt the Reverend was affecting her.

Afterwards, they lay together wordlessly until sleep had nearly come. Then Ramona asked something in a whisper: "Taylor, why would a hotel not have any kind of lock on the front door?" Taylor pondered this in silence and then was asleep.

A couple of hours later, Taylor awoke and looked at the sky and stars framed in the window. He wondered if he was looking at living stars or their ghosts, their nuclear fire having burned out eons ago. Silver moonlight streamed into the room and he thought of the mannequin sleeping dreamlessly in the room down the hall. Suddenly, he sat straight up in bed. "Get up!" he cried, shaking Ramona. "Get up!"

"What? What's going on?"

"Put your clothes on. We're getting the hell out of here."

"Why?" Ramona asked, still trying to wake up. Taylor grabbed her by the arm and lifted her to a sitting position while awkwardly pulling his shorts on with his free hand. She shook her head and said, "Why are we leaving in the middle of the night?"

Taylor was frantically tying his shoes. "Because I know what this place is."

"What?"

"It's a test site for a fucking atomic bomb."

Ramona looked at him in silence for a moment, then was out of the bed and pulling a tee-shirt on.

"That's right," Taylor said. "We're probably lying right in the middle of some strontium-90 cesspool."

They clambered down the stairs. At the front door Ramona paused and caught Taylor by the arm. "Let's leave the Reverend," she said.

"Are you kidding? Leave him out here in the desert? That's just a touch murderous."

"He can make it back to the highway."

"Ramona, get a hold of yourself. There's no way we're leaving him here. He was just crazy drunk. If he was trying to hurt somebody he could have done it."

Before Ramona could reply, Taylor trotted out into the street and kicked the Reverend's foot. He moaned groggily. "Get up, Reverend!"

The Reverend lifted his head and let it fall. "It's still night. What's your problem?"

"You're sleeping right in a fucking radioactive vortex from bomb tests."

That got the Reverend's attention.

They piled into the truck and were soon bouncing across the desert. The Reverend sat beside the window moaning as the truck pounded up and down like a boat. "Pull over. Stop!" he said. He opened the door and vomited lavishly, the smell of semi-digested spam wafting back inside. He pulled the door closed, the truck bounced forward, and at dawn they reached the highway.

By this time everyone's wits had returned, and Taylor had calmed down. "You know, if the place was still hot, we wouldn't have been able to get to it."

"That's true," the Reverend said, "and it had to be on the very periphery of the blast, or however many blasts there were, because it was still standing."

"That's why the first row of buildings leaned away from the desert," Ramona said. "The blast. And that's also why the whole town smelled scorched. It wasn't the desert sun."

"You're right," Taylor said. "And that was the purpose of the mannequins. See what would happen to someone lying in bed, see if the mine would protect the other one. There were probably others here and there in the town that we didn't see. And the bottles in the so-called pharmacy without anything in them. They were wondering if glass would melt. But the blast didn't reach that far. And when the test was over, they examined the town and walked away."

The sun was peeking above the mountain range at their backs as they sped along the highway and Taylor said, "Sure enough. Here it is." On the side of the road, a barbed wire fence appeared, and a mile or so farther there was a labelled gate: United States Military. KEEP OUT.

"Don't you think we should ask someone if that town was still radioactive?" Ramona asked.

"Oh sure," the Reverend replied, "they're going to say they're real sorry that we glow in the dark."

"There's no one to ask anyway," Taylor said. Behind the gate was the usual vista: nothing but desert and distant mountain ranges. But somewhere back there, Taylor knew, there were buildings and bombs. "I really don't think we have anything to worry about," he said. "If they're setting up dummy towns to see what kind of damage the bomb will do, it's because they don't know, and if they don't know, it's probably an early test. I'll bet that town was on the far end of a blast in the fifties. Also, I mean, this is the government. All they have to do is put up a fence if the place is dangerous."

"I guess that's true," Ramona said. She took a deep breath, trying to relax.

Three hours later they pulled onto the Vegas strip.

PART 4

♠

The Mirage had arranged to put Ramona up for the first week, until she could find a place of her own. It was a nice enough perk, though it would have been nicer if they had comped her to one of their own rooms. She would be staying at an inexpensive place off the strip.

Sooner or later one learns that everything in or around a casino is videotaped, and Ramona had learned it a long time ago, so at her insistence Taylor and the Reverend turned off the strip and dropped her off at a taxi stand three or four blocks east. The Reverend let her out and then got back in the truck without a word while Taylor hoisted her bags over the side of the truck bed and set them down beside her on the sidewalk. A couple of winos looked on. She had two suitcases and various paper bags full of stuff. She stood there in the same clothes she had had on the day before, without a bath after the night in the desert, her hair in dirty tendrils around her neck, looking like she belonged with the winos.

It was time to say goodbye. Taylor led her a few yards away from the truck, although the Reverend was paying them no attention anyway.

"So where will you be?" he asked.

"That's something you don't need to know. You don't need to be calling me, and we don't need to be around each other where the wrong people might see us, not for any reason. If you don't know where I am, we can't be around each other," she said. "As soon as I get situated and know I'm on a high limit table, I'll call you."

Taylor and the Reverend were going to try to get a complimentary room at Caesar's, next door to the Mirage, which presumably wouldn't be a problem considering that the Reverend had dropped nine thousand there a month before. If they couldn't get the comp, Taylor would just pay for the room. In any case, that is where they would be.

"If I don't get you the first time," Ramona said, "I'll leave a message saying when I'll call again. Bring the fifty grand when you come to play and buy in for all of it. Might as well get the bosses' attention on the front end, because you're sure going to have it before long. I don't want you digging in your pocket when a good hand's coming. It's best to have the chips there in front of you. Dress well. Look rich. I'll find a reason to quit two days after the game. The next day, three days after, meet me at noon at this little motel over on the west side." She handed him a piece of paper with a little map, scribbled directions, and the name and address of the motel written on it: Lady Luck Motel, Rm. 227.

"Why don't we just meet at Caesar's and have a celebration at their most expensive restaurant?"

Ramona rolled her eyes. "You're a babe in the woods, Taylor. Uh, cameras. Remember? After you win the million, your picture will go from the Mirage to *all* the casinos. They don't like big winners and they watch them. It wouldn't take a particularly sharp surveillance agent at Caesar's to see us together and think that someone over at the Mirage might be interested in this little snip of videotape, you and I partying together. Jesus Christ."

She glared at him for a moment and then her look softened. It was an expression he had not seen since before the trip began. She even allowed herself a little smile. "Have tickets out of here. We can go wherever you want, but I say the Bahamas. They have the game there, and I can get a job dealing. No reason why we shouldn't do it again when the time comes."

Taylor considered the trust she was putting in him. His heart swelled. He would have the entire million for three days. "You're really something," he said, bending to kiss her.

"Yes," she said, offering him her cheek.

As he was getting into the truck he heard her call to him. "Oh, Taylor," she said, "be sure to tip the dealer."

Taylor eased the truck into traffic, and the Reverend asked, "So, are we dumping the bitch?"

"No, no, Reverend."

"Then why are we leaving her on a street corner?—not that it doesn't fit her."

"I told you the Mirage was putting her up until she draws a check."

"So why didn't we take her there?"

Taylor had cooked up an answer for this question during the morning's drive. "She won't be staying at the Mirage. They're putting her someplace else. She's not exactly sure where it is, and I didn't want to get lost looking for it, so she's just gonna give a taxi driver the address."

"I'll give you ten to one that's the last we see of her. She just wanted to get a lift to Vegas and do a little sightseeing on your tab."

"I don't think so, Reverend. She's not like that."

"Oh, she's like that."

"Reverend, what is it about her that you hate so much?"

"She's disrespectful." The Reverend paused, and then added in a guttural tone, "I don't forget it when someone disrespects me." His tone was so cold Taylor felt a chill go up his spine. He glanced over and saw the same look in the Reverend's eye he had seen when he had called Stormy a "harlot." They rode down the strip for a little while and Taylor tried to shake it off. Sometimes the Reverend was like . . . well, sometimes Taylor thought he didn't know enough about him, not enough at all.

Taylor pulled off on a sidestreet and parked. He casually carried the paper bag full of cash like it was something from Walgreen's, and they walked back to the strip and down to the new Bellagio, where Steve Wynn had parked his soon-to-be-sold Renoirs and Picassos. Inside the lobby, Taylor actually paused before making his way to the blackjack pits and looked up for a long moment at the spectacularly strange and beautiful array of Chihuly glass flowers suspended from the ceiling.

At the tables, they sat down at a five dollar shoe game with an automatic shuffler and began to play. After six or seven hands something seemed strange about the way the cards were coming out. "Is this a six deck shoe?" Taylor asked the dealer, a pretty young woman who could have made more money, no doubt, as a cocktail waitress. "Just four decks," she said. On the next hand Taylor watched her put the discards into the shuffler and realized she had done that after every hand. Then she dealt another color-filled hand of face cards and aces. It wasn't that the cards were coming out bad; in fact, he and the Reverend were winning. It was the long and unlikely clump of face cards that was getting Taylor's attention.

"Why are you putting the discards into the shuffler after each hand?" he asked.

"That's just the way we do it here," she said.

"So how do you know when you come to the end of the shoe?"

"You don't come to the end. It's a constant shuffle."

Taylor looked over at the Reverend, then back to the dealer. "I don't get it," he said. "You mean every hand is like the first out of four decks?"

"Yeah, I guess you could look at it like that."

Taylor leaned back in his chair, appalled. "Let's go, Reverend," he said.

The dealer, who knew exactly what the score was, said, "I don't blame you. But you are having some luck."

"That's exactly what it is, and it won't last long," Taylor said.

They got up and left. "It *is* a beautiful place," Taylor said, after he and the Reverend had cashed in a couple of hundred apiece and pushed through the marble doors to the Italianate archway that overlooked a huge artificial lake. Steve Wynn hadn't paid for this with luck; he had done it with odds, and he very obviously didn't want players like them at his casino anyway.

They ambled back to Caesar's, where a person on his way inside did not even need to strain himself walking the final stretch. Taylor and the Reverend stepped on the moving walkway, stood still, and were carried along slowly as they passed through more Greek columns beneath gilded arches. A mawkish, faintly European voice coming from hidden speakers informed them that they were entering Caesar's Palace, where absolutely nothing had been left undone for their pleasure. Taylor looked behind him at the naive, eager faces of the middle-aged couples bearing luggage coming to check in . . . nothing had been left undone for them except the pleasure of having some money left when they finished their weekend junkets from Muncie or Peoria. It was all a racket. He looked at the burnished standards and the Byzantine tapestries on the walls. From Caesar's to the Bahamas to the fucking French Riviera, a sow in a silk dress was still a pig.

They arrived at the entrance to the casino, opened the door, and the fruity European tones gave way to something like the roar of the crowd in a football stadium. Gamblers were wall to wall as far as he could see in the cavernous room beneath the mezzanine on which they stood, looking down over an expanse of table games and slot machines, every last one of them down to the thousandth with a person sitting in front of it, and the clanging of the machines was mixed with the hoots of winners and the groans and curses of losers. Somewhere in the distance, a machine kept up a constant dinging. Someone had hit a jackpot.

Taylor had seen, late one night in Tunica, a dowdy, middle-aged woman win a million dollar jackpot. She had come running into the restaurant where her mother, an ancient white-headed old lady, was eating at the table next to Taylor. "Mom, Mom!" she said. "I just won a million dollars!" That was something to be able to say, Taylor reflected.

They rode down the escalator and found a single deck game that initially looked playable, and the next thing he knew Taylor was deep into it. The cards were not. Or at least the bitch dealer wasn't—on high counts, she cut the deck short, on low counts she kept dealing. But no matter what the count, Taylor was always looking at a stiff, and the Reverend was finding exotic ways to bust: soft seventeen to twelve, twelve to thirteen, thirteen to sixteen, sixteen to twenty six. They dropped a thousand, which made an even ten for the Reverend—counting the nine thousand from last month—and he asked for a room, presenting his player's card to the floor person. The well-dressed young woman with the kind of demeanor that used to be associated with airline stewardesses took the card to the computer. In a minute she was back with an even brighter smile and a complimentary suite. Nothing was too good for a couple of high-rolling losers.

Taylor went back for the truck and soon enough a bellman was piling their "luggage," duffle bags and paper bags—all except the bag Taylor was carrying—onto a cart. They followed the bellman through the lobby, onto the elevator, and to their rooms. Inside the suite, Taylor tipped the man a ten and they took stock of the rooms: a sitting room to begin with . . . a bedroom with a double bed raised on a dais, looking not unlike a bier, Taylor thought . . . a bathroom with a pedestal sink of black marble and a matching jacuzzi . . . another bedroom on the other side with a red satin comforter . . . a sitting room beyond that opened onto a balcony overlooking the strip.

"Not bad for free," Taylor said.

"Not great for ten grand," the Reverend replied. "But we'll get that back. We will, won't we?"

Taylor paused and looked out over the strip while the Reverend waited. Very slowly, he said, "We can't lose."

"Glad to hear it." The Reverend looked down. "Sometimes I get worried. This is a hell of a way to make a living."

"Beats working," Taylor said. "C'mon, man, let's get a shower and get on back to the tables."

They walked out onto the balcony. Night had fallen. The lights of the strip beneath them blazed like a bright future. Beyond them, out on the desert, it was as dark as it had always been.

"I don't know," the Reverend said. "I guess I'm just tired of looking at sixteens that I can't hit without busting, sixteens the dealer fucking cannot bust when he has them. This would be a hell of a place to wind up tapped out . . . let's cut the stakes down for a while until the cards turn our way."

"Your call, Reverend. We were only playing high for the comp. Now that we've got it we'll go to the ten dollar tables . . . hell, the nickel tables. It doesn't matter to me."

Taylor, after all, was biding his time, but the Reverend didn't know that. Still, there was something about the Reverend's dark cloud that was affecting Taylor. Maybe they *should* play the nickel tables and only the nickel tables until Ramona got situated. Taylor knew, or at least he knew on occasion, that he was perfectly capable of getting into a fury and losing a lot of money. A lot. It would be utter stupidity to go into the game with Ramona without a reasonable stake. He thought of how he had been down twenty thousand in the practice game. For a moment Taylor debated with himself about telling the Reverend the plan, but he knew that Ramona would very likely get wind of it, and that would be the end of things. Of course, if she didn't find out until after the game, things would have ended anyway.

Two days of tedious nickel bets later, on excruciatingly slow tables full of novice tourists, Taylor was relaxing in the room when he got the call. "Tomorrow night about eight o'clock," she said and hung up.

The Reverend was in the shower. Taylor immediately called Stormy. "Meet me the day after tomorrow at noon in the Italian restaurant at the Mirage. Start getting ready to go. We'll leave a few days after."

"I'm so excited," she said. "And they have craps down there, right?"

Taylor sighed. "Yes, little lady, you can't win but you can roll the dice as long as you like." Then he brightened, remembering that, after all, she would probably be playing with someone else's money. "You'll be getting eight the hard way," he said, with a leer in his voice.

"Not six?" she said, giggling.

"Well, certainly not four."

"Glad to hear it. When I meet you at the Mirage you'll tell me exactly when we're leaving?"

"Yes. I'll have everything arranged."

"Oh, Taylor, I'm so excited."

"Me too. I'll see you then, sweet thing."

The following evening he explained to the Reverend that they needed to scout the town for a decent game: the Reverend would go downtown and see what was happening at the Horseshoe, find out whether Binion still had a fair game or if he too had changed to something like what they had seen at the Bellagio. Taylor would take the strip. "It's time for us to find a game, Reverend," Taylor said.

The Reverend left with more spring in his step than he had been showing. Perhaps Taylor's repressed anticipation was infectious. With Ramona's admonition in mind to look wealthy, Taylor put on the suit he had bought surreptitiously the day before in one of the shops on the strip; he had decided that his own had become threadbare, and so purchased a gray pin stripe Brooks Brothers as costly as his purse could buy, rich, not gaudy, then gangstered it up with a red shirt and black silk tie so he would look as much mafioso as to the manor born. He wanted to look rich and reckless, more pimp than professor.

The pit bosses were always capable of shutting him down if they thought, or found it expedient to think, that he was a card counter.

He put fifty thousand dollars, save a few thousand in his coat pockets, into a new leather briefcase and walked onto the strip. If the cards were disastrously aberrant, he might need nearly all of it before they turned. He walked down the sidewalk beneath the statues atop columns, stood and looked up at the rearing horses gleaming in spotlights, the gilded chariot containing Caesar himself in heroic pose, and it was all marble and gold, an absolute statement as to which way the money had gone in this game, a gloating taunt to the unending parade of suckers who had come here and would continue to come as long as hope could be packaged and sold.

He would have the Mirage pay him with a check, so the walk back in the middle of the night would not be as dangerous as it might be with cash. Nobody knew what he had on him now. When he started winning, he would certainly draw a crowd. He saw himself in five or six hours stepping out lightly, very lightly indeed, in spite of the weight of a fucking million dollar check, but at the side entrance to the Mirage, where he would soon walk by his favorite thing in Las Vegas, the white tigers, he paused, looking at his reflection in the glass doors. Suddenly, something inside him turned and he stopped cold. He listened down inside himself and heard an alarm. Could he and Ramona really get away with this?

The surveillance people at the Mirage were not novices. There would be experts watching Ramona and him through the cameras from the jump, and then there would be others hovering over them. This wasn't like Tunica—a brand new operation with surveillance personnel and floor supervisors who barely knew how to play blackjack. Many of the Mirage's staff had been in the profession their entire lives, and they were good, probably better than he could imagine.

He remembered the crowd of suits that had gathered around the table that afternoon in Tunica, stone-faced as they watched Ramona push more and more of the casino's money his way. Could she have gotten away with that in Vegas? Here at the Mirage, perhaps the sharpest surveillance people in the world would be watching him, watching her, and when he started to win big, there would be more of them, watching more and more closely.

Well, Ramona believed they could get away with it. She had more to lose than he did. He, after all, could plead ignorance. No, he had no idea why this dealer would cheat for him. None at all. Didn't realize she was doing it.

He stood there with his hands in his pockets, feeling the heft of the bills. It was enough already. He could turn around right now, go back to Memphis, and start a little business. Carpet cleaning, resumé writing, some shit. Make an honest living. He really didn't care to go to prison again. That much was certain. If Ramona bobbled a card, it was all over. What was he thinking? No one would believe he wasn't in collusion with her. It would be a simple matter to find the connection between them back in Tunica. A phone call.

He couldn't make himself step inside. People parted and passed around him as if he were a pole . . .

He remembered a quiet middle-aged man who used to play every day at *Splash*, the first casino in Tunica. The man had a vaguely familiar face and one day it came to Taylor: he owned a well-known restaurant in Memphis. Taylor recognized him from the restaurant and from advertisements. Now, Taylor thought of the man's stoic expression as he took huge losses, and the shrugs of the pit bosses as those losses mounted. One afternoon, Taylor watched him lose twenty thousand dollars and do a creditable job of being a good sport about it.

One day Taylor saw that the restaurant had gone out of business. It had been around for thirty years. Taylor thought of the shrugs, the sly grins between the floor supervisors as the man had shoveled his money out. To hell with them.

He looked at his reflection in the glass doors of the Mirage and squared his shoulders. He smoothed his hair with his hands and looked at himself until he could feel his confidence rising, taking control. He raised his chin. Half a million dollars, give or take what he would leave the Reverend. *Half a million dollars.* That was his share. He and Stormy in the Caribbean where he could play for years, maybe the rest of his life. The Reverend with a decent stake, thirty or forty thousand to do with as he pleased. Ramona with her half to sweeten the bitter pill of his desertion. Everybody happy, or happy enough. *Five hundred thousand dollars.* Enough to keep playing until he beat them on his own terms.

Stormy was young enough to have children. A happy little family on the beach, the two children running in and out of the surf or playing in the sand. An afternoon walk beside the sea, then back to their place on the beach, shanty or villa, that shone with yellow light after the sun went down. A home.

He pushed through the doors. The blackjack pits lay to the left of this entryway. He negotiated his way around tray-carrying waitresses who were squeezing their blown-up busts between blue-haired old women who simply stopped to look around in the middle of streams of people, losers who stomped out so furiously that he had to dodge them, and foreign tourists wearing looks of either studied casualness or wonder, jabbering away in Spanish or Japanese or Czechoslovakian. This wasn't exactly the atmosphere for a card counter, but counting would not be necessary tonight.

In any case, as he approached the blackjack pits the crowd was quieter. The Mirage had a lot of games, and they had been rearranged since the last time Taylor was in town. He spotted a sign advertising the single deck games. He approached a row of high limit tables, where very beautiful Asian or European women with elegant accents chatted with the dealers. He paused behind a table where a couple of grim-faced Arabic men in turbans were betting orange thousand dollar chips, and watched one stand on fifteen against an ace. He had never been able to understand why anyone would bet that kind of money on a game he didn't know how to play, and walked on in disgust.

He passed "reserved" notices on a couple of the tables with thousand dollar minimum signs where the dealers stood stock-still like palace guards, waiting for their mano-à-mano clients, and noted waitresses even bustier than those condemned to serve the rabble and the slot players. These waitresses looked like film stars carrying trays of drinks with a ballet dancer's grace, then leaning to serve them with a stripper's flash. Taylor scanned five or six games, and there she was, Ramona, standing absolutely still behind an empty table.

Their eyes met. Her expression was cold, noncommittal, just as it had been the first time he had ever seen her in Tunica. The sign at the table was purple, and stated "$500 minimum. $25,000 maximum." Taylor walked to the table, nodded to her as he would to any strange dealer, and sat down in the first position. Ramona asked "How are you tonight, sir?" and began to shuffle the cards.

Taylor reached into his pockets and put his money on the green felt. He pushed the bills, hundreds and five hundreds, across the line to

Ramona, and she began to count, turning each bill over and spreading them on the table for the benefit of the cameras above. None of the floor supervisors had yet paid any attention. Then he opened the briefcase and pulled out the rest. When Ramona called out, "Changing fifty thousand," three of them immediately approached the table and looked over her shoulder, confirming the amount of the bills which were elaborately fanned out in groups of ten in front of her. When all three were satisfied, the pit boss said, "Send it," and smiled at Taylor. Taylor returned the smile as casually as he could while Ramona pushed him orange and purple chips and dropped fifty thousand dollars of hard cash down the "hole," a small safety deposit box attached to the table.

Ramona held out the cards and Taylor tucked the yellow card in for his cut just beneath the line of her red, lacquered nails. She reversed the cards and held them ready to deal, waiting for his bet. Her thumb on the deck in her hand was pointing to his left. Taylor reached for his chips and for a moment his hand sat motionless on top of them. This wasn't practice time any longer. He hesitated—could he really bet this much on a hand of blackjack?—but this was it, the chance of a lifetime. He had to keep in mind that this was just another game of blackjack, after all, and it was a game he was bound to win. He put out five orange chips, five thousand dollars.

The cards flipped from Ramona's hands over the stack of thousand dollar chips as if in a dream, falling face down at his fingertips. Ramona turned a ten over. Taylor picked up his cards, looked at them, and snapped then down on the table. Blackjack! Ramona turned over her down card to show twenty, put the discards in the rack, and shoved seventy-five hundred dollars in chips to Taylor. "Good start," she said casually. He smiled and looked at the deck in her hand. Her thumb was on the left. He bet another five thousand.

He looked at two black kings, twenty, and tucked them under his chips. Ramona had an eight up, turned over a five, and just as she prepared to hit Taylor felt his stomach tighten. He always felt it coming when it was too late. Sure enough. There it was: an eight. "Shoot," Ramona said lightly, as she turned over his twenty and raked in his five thousand. "And I thought you were living right," she said. The supervisors who had gathered behind her offered Taylor sympathetic smiles. He shrugged and looked at the deck in Ramona's hand. Thumb on the left. There were only nine tens remaining in the forty three cards she had in her hand, but he supposed she might have access to two of them. He bet five thousand.

Once again he looked at twenty, a red queen and a red jack. Ramona had a deuce up. She turned over an eight and hit with an ace: twenty one. Taylor glanced at the look of shock in her eyes. Well, both of them had known that shit would happen on occasion. This kind of bad luck would make the win look plausible. "Come on, cards," he said. "That's two twenties in a row I've lost."

"Yep," Ramona said grimly. Now her thumb was on the right. Bad hand coming. Taylor pulled back to five hundred, as little as he could bet on this table. He looked at sixteen against a six, stood, Ramona turned over an eight and hit with a three for seventeen. After she gathered the discards and tucked them away, he looked at the cards in her hand. Another bad one coming. He bet five hundred and lost again.

"Maybe you need to tip the dealer," she said jokingly. Her thumb was back on the left. Good hand. But now he was gun-shy. He put out only a thousand and a purple five hundred dollar chip out for her. He looked at ace/eight, or nineteen, against a five up. Ramona turned over a ten, hit it with an ace to sixteen, then with a six to bust. She paid his bet, then her own, saying "Thank you very much, sir," and placed a thousand dollars in her tip box.

Tipping a dealer by placing a bet for him or her, needless to say, encourages cheating, and the winning hand seemed to get the supervisors' attention. They crowded around the table a little more closely, watching Ramona's hands as she slapped the remaining deck together with the discards and began to shuffle.

Taylor smiled inwardly. It wasn't the way she shuffled, after all. It was the way she could pick and choose which cards to deal. She held the cards out to him, and he made the cut. He was down four thousand. So what? The cards pointed the right way. He bet five thousand.

He looked at ace/eight, or nineteen, against an eight. He stood, knowing that Ramona would turn over a ten for eighteen. She turned over a deuce for ten and Taylor gasped, feeling his stomach tighten. The inevitable ten followed and Ramona whisked away five thousand-dollar chips, slapping them in the rack with the same awful finality he remembered so well.

It was beginning to look like a bad start. Not a problem. After all, it had taken an hour to get moving during the practice session in the desert. Ramona was able to know what his cards would be, and was giving him good hands. She was perhaps able to know one of her cards also, but she could not know the second one, and the house was getting very lucky. It could not last. The cards in her hand were once again indicating a good hand for Taylor. Five thousand again.

She dealt him eight/three and turned up a five. A classic situation where nearly every rank novice knows to double his bet. Taylor hesitated and looked up at her face. The three supervisors, one over her shoulder, two on the ends of the table standing slightly back but close enough to see both his expression and hers, watched them closely. Her expression remained entirely impassive, but her thumb on the cards shifted slightly to the right. A good card. Taylor put out five thousand more to double. She tucked the card face down beneath his chips and turned over her card. A ten, as it should have been. "Now hit that fifteen without busting," Taylor taunted, challenging the odds. Dutifully, she turned over a six for twenty-one. Taylor groaned, and one of the supervisors echoed him with mock sympathy.

He still had a chance to push. Ramona turned over his down card. A nine, yet. Twenty. He had just lost ten thousand dollars on the hand. "How am I losing all these twenties?" Taylor asked of anyone who could answer him. Ramona shrugged. It was her old persona in spades. "Just the way the cards fall," she said.

Then a little coquettish smile played across her lips. "Remember that it improves your luck to tip the dealer," she said. One of the supervisors scowled. Hustling tips is forbidden. But Taylor indicated with a light expression that it didn't bother him, and the supervisor said nothing. The cards in her hand were indicating a good hand coming, but he was gun-shy again. Until this streak of house luck played itself out, he had better be conservative. He bet a thousand for himself, five hundred for Ramona. A king and queen showed up in his hand for twenty. Ramona had a ten up. Taylor's stomach tightened as she turned over her down card, but it was only an eight for a standing eighteen.

It was about time he won a hand. However, since he had given away five hundred on the dealer bet, as it were, he had won only five hundred dollars. Winning that and losing ten thousand wasn't going to make it, and now the cards in Ramona's hand indicated a bad hand. He lost on a couple of stiffs at five hundred apiece and rode out the deck. He had lost over ten thousand on the round, putting him down nearly twenty thousand dollars.

"Well, I've played through two decks and I'm down twenty grand," he said to Ramona.

"Maybe this third one will be better," she replied. The cards in her hand were pointed the correct way. Her expression was impassive, but as he put out his bet she said, "Remember, you're only winning when you're tipping."

"Oh yeah," Taylor said, pretending to go along with the superstition of it. After all, these tips were basically trivial when set against a million dollars. He bet five thousand this time, and put out five hundred for the dealer. Ramona dealt the cards. "Yes!" he cried, and tossed down another sparkling blackjack on the green felt table.

"See, I can be bought," Ramona said, laughing.

"Yeah, but you're not cheap," Taylor replied.

She paid him seventy five hundred, and herself twelve hundred and fifty, really, because when he bet for her, she was winning not only the payoff on the bet but the original bet as well.

He remembered a morning as the sun was rising in Tunica, and he had found himself playing at a table with a drunken woman who bet a dollar for the dealer on every hand, while she herself bet five. The woman had been playing all night and was down eight hundred dollars. Since she had played at least eight hundred hands, it was very easy to see that what she had lost was precisely the dollars she had bet for the dealer. Otherwise, she would have been about even. At the time, Taylor had had to stop himself from pointing this out to her, since the dealer would not have appreciated it.

Now Ramona's hands were pointing the correct way again. The blackjack had given him confidence, and Taylor bet ten thousand. It was time to start winning. Ramona dealt the cards, and Taylor was surprised to see himself looking at a seventeen. But she had a five up. That was what she was going to do: bust herself. She turned over a ten. "OK, OK, you can do it," Taylor said. *Please, God,* he said to himself, *don't let this happen to me.* She turned over a three for eighteen. "I can't bust," she said in disbelief. The supervisors sighed, a little Greek chorus of sympathy for Taylor. Taylor knew they were chuckling under their breath.

He felt cold fury rising. He could not possibly lose with the advantage he had. The house simply could not get perfect cards, or cards just good enough to beat him, when Ramona was picking and choosing at least half the cards. It could not happen. His luck could not be this bad.

They traded five thousand dollar hands until she was shuffling again. He made the cut. Her thumb on the deck was pointing, as had been the case on every first hand, the correct way. He bet five thousand and drew a ten and a king, twenty, against a deuce. Ramona turned over another deuce, hit with a three, a third deuce, a seven to sixteen, and then slapped down a five with a disgusted roll of her eyes for twenty-one. Incensed, Taylor pounded his fist on the table. "I haven't won a fucking twenty yet," he said, practically shouting. "What's going on here?"

Ramona shrugged, but the implications of what Taylor might be saying got the supervisors' attention, and their eyes narrowed. "Sometimes it just isn't your day," the pit boss said. "Maybe you ought to take a break."

"Fuck a break," Taylor said. He was barely able to control himself. The pit boss seemed to sense this, and apparently decided not to pursue the ban on obscenities that every casino has. It was quite possible, given a little nudge, that Taylor's anger might have found a focus. As it was, he could only be angry at fate. The pit boss and the two henchmen beside him said nothing as Taylor looked at Ramona's deck of cards and pushed out another five thousand.

Ramona dealt him nineteen against a three. She turned over a ten for thirteen and as she was hitting Taylor could feel it. Sometimes players talk about "wearing a stool home." His stomach tightened. "What a surprise," he said with disgust. A seven for twenty. He had seen this kind of dealer streak happen before, and it didn't necessarily stop. The question was, how was it happening when she was choosing, or at least culling, the cards?

Now he had fifteen thousand dollars left. Ramona's cards were pointing toward a good hand. He decided to bet five thousand once more, and if this didn't win, to pull back radically until he started to climb.

Ramona dealt him a pair of aces. She showed a six up. This was a classic split. But he hesitated for a moment. If she had a ten she could get to, and she knew she had a ten down, she could bust herself no matter what she gave him. There had to be a way to win this one even if she didn't give him good cards. He split. She dealt him another ace.

Taylor looked into her eyes. This was it. It would cost him everything he had to split again. But there was no sense of hesitation in her gaze. Almost imperceptibly, she nodded. He shoved his last five thousand in chips out and she split the aces again. Then, in a perfect little ascension, she dealt him a seven, eight, and a nine for eighteen, nineteen, and twenty. Not bad. Not absolutely safe, but not bad. Even if Ramona were not cheating for him, and if there were not fifteen thousand dollars riding on the hand, Taylor would have felt fairly relaxed, because the fact that he had not gotten a ten card meant that the odds were increased that the dealer would, and so would bust.

If he won, he won fifteen thousand dollars. If he lost, he lost that amount. Thus, there were thirty thousand dollars at stake. Ramona took a deep breath and turned over her down card. Taylor gasped.

It was not a ten at all. It was a five. Taylor and Ramona looked at eleven. She hesitated, as if she could not bring herself to deal the last card. The pit boss stepped forward and said, "Deal the cards." Remembering his role as someone "on the player's side," he added, "Maybe it's a little one and you'll bust on the next one." She turned over the card, glanced at it, and threw it down. An ace! "There is a God," Taylor said. Ramona smiled. The next card had to be a ten. She took it from the deck and just dropped it in front of her, where it lay as coldly visible as a dead snake. The cards have no conscience, no heart. But they do have eyes. It was a nine. Twenty-one. Ramona's eyes met Taylor's. He thought he saw a glimmer of disbelief, then she was back in character, simply a cold-hearted dealer with a blank stare who had just taken fifty thousand from a rich gambler.

Stunned, he rose from the table without a word, unable to look at her again or the bosses who stood in a silent pack behind her.

Outside, on the street, Taylor felt furtive, as if he had committed a crime. Something inside him cringed and wanted to hide as laughing people walked past. He checked in his pockets and found a few hundred dollars. That was it. Soon enough he would be broke as only a gambler or a drug addict can be broke, which is to say completely without assets of any kind at all. How could he possibly have lost? He felt like the unluckiest man alive, and he wanted to know why.

The only possible way out of this jam was to meet up with the Reverend and find out what kind of stake he had left. Maybe he had won. Maybe the Reverend would stake him to a few thousand and he could get his money back. Taylor returned to the hotel. In the room, he waited for three hours as he stared out over the lights of Las Vegas, cursing the city for its vanity, its banal dreams.

At last the Reverend's key card slid into the lock and the door swung open. As he stood framed in the doorway Taylor could tell from the slump of his shoulders what had happened. He came into the room and said, "I'm tapped. How did you do?"

"Sit down, Reverend. I have something to tell you."

Taylor took a deep breath and told him the whole story, leaving out only the part that had to do with Stormy. When he was through the Reverend's eyes narrowed and he voiced something that had been playing around the edges of Taylor's consciousness, something even worse than impossibly bad luck.

"Taylor, that bitch cheated you."

"But why, Reverend?"

"For sport."

"That's a long way to go for sport, Reverend. Would it not be more entertaining for her, if you will, to be on her way to the Caribbean?" Since Stormy had been left out of the scenario, the Reverend was getting the same plan Taylor had pitched to Ramona, but even this expurgated version raised the spectre of the Reverend's abandonment.

"So you were just going to leave me here?" he asked.

"With fifty grand, Reverend. Fifty grand."

"Well, that would have eased the pain of your departure, no doubt. Anyway, it's academic now. But why, just out of curiosity, weren't you going to take me with you?"

"Ramona would not have gone if you were going, Reverend."

"At that point, why would you even need the bitch?"

"We were going to keep on keeping on, Reverend. She's a bitch who can deal whatever cards she wants to."

"Listen to what you're saying."

Taylor had already heard himself.

The next day Taylor left the Reverend in the room by saying he was going downstairs to play quarter slot machines and walked over to the restaurant at the Mirage at the appointed hour, thinking that lunch was going to cost him about a third of the money he had left. He avoided walking past the blackjack pits the way he might have avoided a bar where he had drunkenly humiliated himself; furthermore, he didn't want to spook Ramona. He was certain that she would meet him when and where she had said she would. Then she would explain how things had gone so wrong, and give back the tip money, which had now become a significant amount. He did glance furtively at the distant line of tables.

He didn't see her and she probably wasn't there anyway—but who knew what her hours were?

He had no idea how he would play out the situation with Stormy, but he had to inform her that they would not be going to the Bahamas. This wasn't going to be easy. On occasion in the past, when he had been in dire straights, the most unlikely people had helped him. It could be an interesting turn of events if Stormy helped him, staked him until he could get rolling again.

He looked over the heads of the people waiting in line for a table and saw her sitting at a booth near a window. She was sitting on the outside of the booth with her legs crossed. The hemline of a short black cocktail dress rested across her thighs, bless its every lucky thread, and one shoulder strap was actually down around her arm. She looked stunning and wanton. Taylor saw a passing waiter do a double-take, and then became aware that he was one of at least three men in the line craning their heads to look at her. Taylor got the *maitre d's* attention and nodded in Stormy's direction.

"I'm joining her for lunch," he said.

The *maitre d'* looked dubious but led him to the front of the line, looked in Stormy's direction until he got her attention, and then gestured toward Taylor. Stormy smiled and nodded, and Taylor was waved toward her. He felt the eyes of the men in line on his back.

"How are you doing?" she asked as he sat down.

"Up and down," he answered. "Too many dealers won't go deep anymore."

"Silly," she said, and covered his hand briefly with hers. "I don't mean at the tables. I mean in general."

"Oh," Taylor said. "Well, I guess I've been okay."

"You don't look like you mean that." Her tone was sympathetic, almost cloying.

He thought, cynically, that it was amazing how a trip to the Bahamas could bring out the caring part of a woman, and then he said just that.

Stormy didn't miss a beat. "Oh, you," she said playfully. "A trip doesn't hurt but what brings it out is time for a person to think about who she's really interested in."

"Why did you tell the Reverend that I made a pass at you?"

"God, are you gonna start that again? I thought we had it all cleared up." She paused for a second, looking petulant. "Okay, listen up and I'll tell you again. I was confused. I was upset because I was supposed to be with the Reverend but I was attracted to you. I guess maybe I wanted him to send me to you."

"But you just left. Why didn't you call me?"

"I wanted to, Taylor. I really did. But like I said, I was confused. Something told me not to, something told me maybe you were regretting what you said."

"I've never really regretted telling the truth, although I must admit I had some second thoughts once the Reverend got wind of it."

"The Reverend," Stormy snorted derisively. "I can't believe I was ever interested in him."

"Who've you been seeing out here?"

"Nobody since we got back in touch."

Stormy wasn't very good at deceit. She didn't need to be. A person believes what he wants to believe as long as possible. Some people can do it for a lifetime. For most, though, collisions with the facts force a slight and grudging familiarity with the truth, a condition which can generally be treated with drug therapy or diversionary tactics such as going insane. Had Taylor been twenty years younger, he might have believed her. As it was, he knew she was lying, but chose not to care that she was. What difference did it make?—and why did it not? For the shallowest of reasons. Skin-deep. Taylor knew he was being outright stupid, but couldn't stop himself. Stormy would have turned a blind man's head. Anybody would have thought she was pretty, more than pretty, but for Taylor she was something out of a dream. She was the embodiment of his fantasies.

"Let's get a room," he said. "I can get a comp here for a honeymoon suite."

Stormy laughed. "Taylor, I've got appointments this afternoon. There's a lot to do to get ready to go to the Bahamas."

"There's time," he said.

"No, there's not."

Taylor stared out the window. There was a show going on at the pool. Dolphins leaped and splashed down joyfully, sending sprays of water over the applauding spectators. He remembered Stormy standing above him at his aunt's pool and shaking water on his chest. Somewhere in the distance, one of the Mirage's caged white tigers coughed. He was going to have to tell her.

"Stormy, we're going to have to put off the trip for a while."

Her wine glass stopped halfway to her mouth: "What?"

"We're going to have to put it off for a while."

"How can you say that? I've gone to a lot of trouble to arrange things."

"We have to put it off because I don't have the money right now. You remember the sure thing I told you about? Well, it went wrong."

Stormy looked at him in stunned disbelief. Then she said, "I know just what went wrong. You fucking lost. You lost your money."

"Well, yeah, that's the long and short of it."

"You put me to the trouble of making plans to go with you and then you come out here and in three days lose all your money." Taylor glanced around. She was seething, raising her voice.

"You don't understand." He hesitated for a second but there was little reason to protect Ramona about something that could never be proved against her anyway. He told Stormy the whole story while she squirmed in her seat. When he was through, and hoping for a sympathetic expression, he got even more of a glare.

"I should have known that bitch dealer had something to do with it. In fact, I think I did know it somehow. Listen, I've got to go."

"Stormy, wait, please."

She stood up from the table and her voice was loud: "No, you've got the gall to try to get me in a room with you when you don't have any money, when we're not going anywhere. I don't have time for losers."

And she turned and walked out.

Taylor sat there for a long moment, trying not to feel the stares of the people around him. Then he got up. "What a surprise," he said to no one in particular.

Two long days and nights of nickel games later, Taylor approached the Lady Luck Motel through the meaner streets of West Las Vegas. It was mid-morning and heat waves shimmered over the streets as he surveyed the neighborhood he was passing through. This was hardly the strip. It did not even rise to the level of the environs surrounding the sawdust joints, the smaller gambling places with a couple of table games and ten or fifteen slot machines. In fact, this area did not seem particular to Las Vegas at all, but rather like the industrial outskirts of any city, the place where used car lots give way to piles of tires in weedy lots behind barbed wire. Now and then a bored and hungoverish-looking streetwalker on a corner glanced without much expectation at his passing truck.

He followed Ramona's scribbled directions until it seemed that he was going to leave the city and enter the desert, but at last he saw the motel sign: "Lady Luck Motel" hand-painted above a pair of dice showing seven beside a crudely rendered blackjack on a piece of plywood nailed to a pole. Somehow, he was certain Ramona would be there. The Reverend was wrong, had to be wrong. Taylor and Ramona had quite simply run into the worst luck in the world, and she was about to explain how it had happened. She would give him back some of the tip money, which alone would be enough to get him rolling again.

Or there could be an empty room with no sign of her.

He was fifteen minutes late. She should already be here. He pulled into the parking lot and started looking for Room 227. If she had already arrived there was no point in stopping at the office. He scanned the numbers on the doors. There were three separate buildings, but the far one was the only two story. That had to be it. Behind the building the gun metal-colored mountains loomed in the distance, and the sky behind them was a deep turquoise. He watched the shadow of a cloud cross the mountains and breathed in the heat-seared smell of the asphalt parking lot as he tried to calm himself. Surely she was here . . . there were two or three small, nondescript vehicles that might be rental cars, three or four pick-ups and a ragged old Buick. Then he saw her standing in a doorway on the second floor, looking at him.

He drove toward her and their eyes met for just a second. Then she stepped inside and closed the door behind her. Taylor parked the truck slowly. Could her expression really have communicated what he thought it had? Cold anger? Why would she be angry at him? If anything, it worked the other way. He told himself he had misread her expression and got out of the truck.

He climbed the concrete steps and looked at 227 on the door. For some reason, he considered knocking. That would be ridiculous. He did it anyway. He took a deep breath, knocked a couple of times, and turned the knob. The door swung open.

It took a moment for his eyes to adjust to the darkness inside the room, and then it hit him, something familiar he couldn't identify. A clear sense of foreboding came over him, something like what the first person on a crime scene must feel when he walks into the apartment of the person who doesn't answer the telephone and sees blood on the walls. But Taylor did not see gore or disarray.

She was not in the darkened room, which was lighted only by a couple of candles burning in front of a mirror. He looked across the tightly made bed with an Indian sari draped across it. The bathroom door was closed. Okay, that was where she was. He breathed in the thick scent of incense and saw the stick burning in an ashtray on a bedside table. On the same table, a cheap tape recorder played sitar music which he could barely hear because of the blood pounding in his ears.

He sat down on the edge of the bed, trying to bring to consciousness what this reminded him of, trying to understand why his heart was pounding. Then he leaped to his feet and started toward the bathroom, and by the time he swung the door open he knew what he would find. No doubt someone who did not have the promise of a million dollars clouding his judgment would have known it long before.

A desert breeze fanned the thin white curtain through the open window. He stood on the toilet and peered out. The walkway wrapped around here just below the window, as if the construction plans had been changed as to which way the rooms would face. There was no sign of Ramona. Then he stepped back to the floor, and saw it sitting there on the back of the toilet: a note, folded in half, written on the blank card that comes at the front of a new deck. On the outside he saw "Taylor." He unfolded it and read, in a florid script, "I see hard luck coming for you, gambler."

PART 5

♠

The next morning Taylor and the Reverend were at Caesar's playing video poker. Tedious but cheap. "We're gonna find that bitch and have a few words with her," the Reverend said.

"What is there to say, Reverend? The money's gone."

"She's got over three grand of your tip money. That's in her pocket, and we need it."

Taylor knew that this was true, but confronting Ramona didn't appeal to him, particularly in the casino where all the muscle was behind her. It would be insane to threaten her, and the Reverend might try anything. If there was any trouble, they would be thrown out or possibly arrested . . . and they wouldn't be able to make bail.

"We need to find out where she lives, Reverend. We can't approach her in the casino. She'll just make it look like I'm a sore loser."

"We'll sit down at her table and start playing. Real quiet. Never take our eyes off her and never say a word. In a few minutes she'll be begging to give you back your money."

"We don't have the stakes to play at her table. Hundred dollar minimum."

This gave the Reverend pause for just a moment. Then he said, "Then we'll just stand behind the table and watch, like novices. The suits will think we're learning the game, or yokels gawking at the high rollers. But we'll just stare at that bitch."

Taylor didn't like it. He didn't have much stomach for this kind of thing. Not his style . . . still, they had to do something. They had to have money to play.

An hour later, Taylor and the Reverend entered the casino with Taylor trying to keep the latter in tow, keep him toned down. The Reverend looked grim and purposeful, and Taylor could see that they would not be inconspicuous standing near the table. The expression the Reverend had on his face would draw suits immediately. Taylor grabbed him by the shirtsleeve.

"Look, Reverend, you need to cool down. If you go near the blackjack pits with this attitude, we're gonna get tossed."

The Reverend considered this, letting the observation sink in. Then he shook himself, looked down, and came back up with an innocuous grin. "How's this?" he asked.

"Better. Now keep it that way. Just our presence will rattle her, you can he sure of that."

They approached the high rolling pit and looked around. Ramona was nowhere to be seen. "Maybe she's on break, or maybe this is her day off," Taylor said.

"I wonder," the Reverend replied.

Taylor approached the table where he had played and lost. The pit boss greeted him effusively, thinking that Taylor was back to lose more. "Where's the dealer I played against the other night?" Taylor asked. "I want to get my money back from her."

"Oh, yeah, the new woman. What was her name? Just a minute, I'll see if she's on tonight." The man walked away and talked to a couple of other suits. Then he returned and said, "She quit a couple of days ago, I guess. Made a paycheck and hasn't shown up since."

The Reverend leaned in and asked, "Do you know where she lives?" For obvious reasons, the pit boss was not very likely to give out that kind of information. His eyes narrowed and he said stiffly, "No, I don't, and if I did I couldn't tell you."

The Reverend's face turned to stone. This was an unacceptable answer. As soon as Taylor saw his expression, he grabbed him by the arm and led him away from the tables. The Reverend moved reluctantly, but in a minute they were lost in the crowds milling through the maze of slot machines.

"We've got to find that bitch," the Reverend said.

"We need to figure out another way."

Both of them were quiet for a while. Taylor started absently putting quarters in a slot machine while the Reverend pondered the reels, lost in thought. "You don't know a single person she's connected to? No friends or family?"

"I never heard her mention either one. I'm pretty sure her parents are dead, or at least dead to her. Friends? Ramona? I don't think so. Hey—wait a minute—have you used that telephone since she called me?"

"What telephone?"

"The one in the hotel room."

"I ordered room service a couple of times."

"That doesn't matter. What's important is whether or not anybody has called us. Has the phone rung at all?"

"I don't think so. Who would call us?" Suddenly, the Reverend's eyes lit up.

"That's right," Taylor said. "We might still be able to star-sixty-nine the call."

They were trotting toward the door and then down the sidewalk momentarily. Caesar's didn't give you a ride out.

Back in the room at the Mirage, Taylor picked up the receiver and dialed *69. A robotic voice informed him that the last incoming call was received on July 23 at 8:15 p.m. from 767-6540. That was it. That was her call. Taylor dialed the number and someone, possibly a guest, possibly an employee, picked up a lobby phone and spoke two words which that person would never know had sealed a woman's fate: "Lovelace Motel.

They located the little motel quickly, and the desk clerk informed them, for a price of fifty dollars, that one Ramona Richards had checked out an hour earlier, leaving a forwarding address for Ely, Nevada. When they approached the truck the Reverend jumped into the driver's seat. "Give me the keys," he said. "You drive so slow we'll never catch up with her." Cursing the delay but thinking of the scarcity of gas stations, the Reverend bought and filled a couple of five gallon cans and put them into the back of the truck. Soon enough they were out of town and speeding past the sign that said "Highway 150, the Loneliest Highway in America." The Reverend pushed the truck to the limit and the speedometer wavered around 110. For nearly an hour they saw no one at all, and then in the distance a dot appeared: another car. It would disappear as the road crossed over a mountain range, then reappear as the road leveled out. It was perhaps two or three miles ahead. Taylor found it difficult to judge the distance, because he was unused to being able to see so far on dry land. The terrain gave one the same sense of space that the ocean does. But soon enough it was evident that they were gaining on the car. After about thirty minutes they were close enough to see that a woman was driving.

Taylor felt an intense misgiving. Somehow, he knew it was her. He looked over at the Reverend, who was peering ahead with a clenched jaw. It was time to tell the truth before things got out of hand. "You know, Reverend, I haven't really told you the whole story." And he told him about Ramona being aware from the computer exchanges of his plans to leave her behind. He told him of his plans to take Stormy with him instead. The Reverend appeared to take this stoically, given his priority with the girl. Then Taylor added, "Ramona didn't know I was going to give her half the money. She thought I was going to double-cross her, so she screwed me. She gave me the money to begin with. Then she took it back. What kind of man would I be if I didn't grant her just a little respect for getting even?"

"You'd be the fucking coward that you are, that's what kind. We are going to catch up with this double-crossing bitch, and we're gonna get back what she has of our money. And that's every penny she has. Period."

The blood rose in Taylor's face as he tried to convince himself that the Reverend had not just called him a coward, that the Reverend was not getting ready to rob a woman who had done nothing to him, who had done very little to Taylor other than take back the money she had given him, and done that because she believed he was going to steal all of what she intended to share with him.

The Reverend held the gas pedal to the floor but the speedometer seemed stuck. The truck would go no faster. The car ahead was streaking along at a similar pace, but they continued to gain almost imperceptibly. If Ramona was giving it everything the little rental car had, the truck had a little more, and they finally came alongside her in the passing lane. Slowly, very slowly, her profile came into view. "That's her," the Reverend said. She glanced over at Taylor, met his eye, and immediately looked back to the road.

The Reverend began honking and gesturing for her to pull over. She kept driving, with her jaw set and all her attention on the road. The Reverend got a bit ahead and jogged the truck slightly into her lane, as if he would knock her off the road, but she still kept driving. Taylor kept trying to catch her eye again and give her some indication that they didn't mean to hurt her. The Reverend eased off just a bit and then they were speeding side by side again. Taylor barely had time to register the Reverend's arm moving and then the .38 appeared and there was a huge explosion two inches in front of his face.

The driver's window of Ramona's car blew out in a thousand pieces and her car careened off the road and into the desert at one hundred miles per hour. Taylor turned around in his seat to look and tried to hold on while the Reverend stomped on the brakes. Ramona's car bounced across furrows in the sand while scattering cacti into the air, then left the ground and spun sideways, like a top, two or three times. Incredibly, the car stayed right-side up and did not roll. When the truck finally skidded to a stop, the Reverend threw it into reverse and they backed alongside where Ramona had come to rest inside a billowing cloud of fine dust.

The Reverend jumped out of the truck carrying the gun. Taylor got out screaming for him to put it down. The Reverend just kept walking toward the car, and Taylor ran ahead of him to shield Ramona. When they got close to the car, Taylor could see Ramona's shoulders shaking and then, through the ringing in his ears that still sounded from the shot, he could hear her sobbing. She looked up at them through tears, but her expression was defiant. "She's got guts. That much is certain," Taylor thought. If he could convince Ramona that he was on her side, not the Reverend's, maybe together they could stop the maniac.

"Get out of the car, bitch," the Reverend said, and pointed the gun at her face. Taylor stood still as Ramona stared levelly into the barrel of the .38 and slowly began to unbuckle her seatbelt and unfold herself out of the car. She was shaken but unhurt. The bullet had missed her head and blown out the window on the other side as well. She stood up straight and looked from the Reverend to Taylor.

"You were going to ditch me and take that slut with you."

"Yes, but"—

"Shut up!" the Reverend screamed. "I don't care about this shit. We want the tip money and everything else you have."

"My purse is in the car," Ramona said.

"Reach in there and get it."

Ramona leaned into the car. Taylor watched the Reverend's hand on the gun. This sort of strong-arm robbery was not exactly what he had bargained for. He looked away, and when he did he saw an old cattle truck in the distance, coming toward them.

"Reverend, look," he said, nodding toward the truck.

The Reverend saw it and took stock. "They're gonna stop and see if we need any help out here in the sand. We have to get out of here." He pushed Ramona into the passenger seat and said to Taylor, "I'll drive this. You get in the truck and follow."

Before Taylor had time to think the Reverend had the car spitting sand behind it and fishtailing toward the road. The little car bounced onto the asphalt and Taylor trotted toward the truck. Soon enough he was following them and thinking that this had now become a kidnapping. In his rearview mirror, now so far back that it looked like the toy a person sees from a plane, Taylor watched the cattle truck turn off the highway onto one of the roads to nowhere.

It was clear to Taylor that whatever was happening had to stop. He honked and motioned for the Reverend to pull over. They would not take all of Ramona's money. They would merely take enough—or ask for enough—to give them a decent chance at the cheap tables until they recouped. He would explain to Ramona that that was all they needed . . . a chance. He would smile, would say that he had no hard feelings, would wave her on her way. He and the Reverend would drive back to Vegas and find a three-dollar table. It would be a long climb back, but they were in it for the long haul anyway.

The Reverend would not pull over. Taylor honked again, and the Reverend sped up. Where was he going? There was nothing Taylor could do now but follow, and so settled in behind. They drove for an hour . . . two hours. The desert sun passed over the top of the truck and began to shine on the side of his face.

Suddenly, the Reverend slowed down. What? Taylor had been driving so long without touching the brakes that he nearly rear-ended the rental car. He veered to the left with his tires squealing and had to back up to make the turn the Reverend was making. This road to nowhere seemed familiar, and then he recognized it: the road to the ghost town. Why were they going there? Taylor honked in desperation but the Reverend drove on without even glancing back. They drove over the tracks they had left the week before. There were no others.

Taylor watched the Reverend skid to a stop in front of the hotel and then saw him roughly push Ramona out. Taylor threw the truck into park and got out as Ramona stumbled and fell in the dirt, then picked herself up and brushed off a little tartan skirt she was wearing with a white blouse. She was dressed like a college girl but the expression on her face didn't look like a college girl's: through her tough bitch glare just a hint of fear was showing.

Taylor glanced at the Reverend and knew that things could get even worse. "Hold on, Reverend," he said. "Just calm down. Now, Mona, we need a little of my tip money, just enough"— he stopped short when he saw the Reverend raise the gun in his hand and point it directly at his forehead.

"You shut up. I'll handle this," the Reverend said. When he was certain that Taylor was in complete agreement he turned back to Ramona. "Give me all of your money, right now, or I'm going to kill you and find it myself," the Reverend said. Taylor knew that he meant it.

At such moments, a person *sees* a silent screen. The eyes widen and the pupils dilate, while it is probably blood pounding in the ears that obscures other sound. Here in the desert there was hardly a sound anyway, not even a breeze to make the hotel sign creak and waft away the clouds of dust their vehicles and Ramona's falling had raised. But Taylor could see every pore and freckle on the hand that held the gun. It was like the moment the Reverend had mentioned in his sermon regarding the count and the cards, that hour late in the day when the sun is at just the right angle and hits the lake where one has been fishing, the water that has been opaque becomes translucent, and suddenly one can see; suddenly something large and dark moves near the bottom. Taylor felt like he was seeing his partner clearly for the first time. The Reverend pointed the gun at Ramona's chest and Taylor watched the tendons in his wrist tighten.

"I'll get you the money," Ramona said.

"You do that," he said, motioning with the gun.

Once again, Ramona leaned into the car. This time she came out with her purse, pulled out her wallet and started toward the Reverend.

"Just toss it," he said.

She threw it to him underhanded. The Reverend caught it, pulled out the cash, and dropped the wallet on the ground. He started counting.

"There's only thirty-three hundred dollars here. There should be thirty-five from Taylor alone."

"That's all I have."

"Bullshit. You got Taylor to tip you thirty five hundred. You're saying you didn't get anymore from all the other players at a hundred dollar table? Do I look stupid to you?"

"I only dealt for five days. Do you think dealers make thousands a week? Once in a while I get tipped. Most of the time I get stiffed."

"She's telling the truth, Reverend," Taylor said.

"How the fuck do you know? Pull out your luggage there, two-timer, and start throwing everything on the ground."

"This has gone far enough, Reverend. Leave her alone. Thirty three hundred is more than enough. We don't even need it all. Just take a thousand and let's go back to the city, get a cheap room. I can turn it into something."

"You've been telling me that ever since I've known you. The only money I've seen, this bitch cheated away from us."

"She gave me the money to begin with, Reverend."

"That's right, and you're not gonna win a penny with a thousand dollar stake. Or thirty three hundred. Or a hundred thousand. You're a fucking loser." He turned his attention back to Ramona. "Now come up with the money."

"That's all there is," Ramona shouted. "That's all there is."

The Reverend shot her in the stomach. Taylor felt the concussion of the shot in his chest, like the bass from a huge amplifier. He took a step backward and watched Ramona sink to her knees. She knelt there in front of the Reverend with her fingers knitted over the wound and her head bowed, watching the blood flow through her hands and drip into the dust.

"Where's the money?" the Reverend said.

Ramona turned her gaze up to him. "Okay, okay, I'll get it. You win," she said, as if she were conceding a small argument. There was no need for anyone to get angry. She stood by raising one knee and pushing herself up with both hands. She hesitated for a moment, as if checking her balance, and then turned toward her car and began walking stiffly. A dark red trail followed her.

Suddenly she began to run, rather impressively for how badly she was hurt but really little more than a trot. She was wailing, "There's no more! There's no more!" when the Reverend shot her again in the back. She stumbled and fell face forward at the same moment that Taylor threw himself at the Reverend and knocked the gun out of his hand.

The .38 spun underneath the truck, and Taylor was positioned between it and the Reverend. Taylor dove under the truck to retrieve it, crawled out the other side, and stood up pointing it to where the Reverend had been. But the Reverend, realizing that he had no chance at getting to the gun before Taylor did, had already ducked around the corner. Taylor turned his attention to Ramona.

She had dragged herself up the steps to the walkway and was halfway inside the door to the hotel. Taylor ran toward her as she struggled to pull herself inside to some scant hope of safety. Slipping in blood on the walkway, he managed to keep his footing, bent down and pulled her by her arms through the door, then slammed it shut and jammed a chair beneath the doorknob. Ramona was breathing heavily, as if she had run a long way. He again grabbed her beneath her arms and pulled her into the far room, away from the door and the front windows.

Ramona lay flat on her back. She was wearing a red blouse, red skirt, red legs. Taylor knelt beside her. "I've got his gun. We're going to get to the truck and get some help." She looked up at him with cloudy eyes. He knelt beside her and glanced at the pool of blood collecting around her. "This is a dream, Mona," he said. "This is just a dream."

"Hold me, Taylor, for a little while. Pretend that you care about me."

Taylor lay down and cradled her head in his arms. "I care about you."

"You were going to take the money and run off with that slut. You were going to leave me behind after what I had done for you."

"I was going to give you half the money, Mona." He looked at her, grabbed her up and shook her by the shoulders. "I was going to give you half the money, Mona!" he shouted into her face. She did not hear him.

Taylor let her head fall back to the floor gently but quickly. She felt strange. He did not want to touch her. Looking was different, and he looked intently. He felt something curious deep inside, something like admiration: she had just done the hardest thing anyone can do. He searched her face for an expression. It was beyond expression.

It had all been sort of a game, really, from the time he met her until this moment. A game of disguises, shadowy ghosts taking shape inside a computer. Now it was real. He thought about the times he had tapped out at the tables. It had never mattered. The cards would still be coming out when he got the money together to play again. Ramona had *lost.* And Taylor knew that it was precisely that loss that now gave her life form and meaning. Only in the end could what had come before be understood.

A shaft of sunlight broke on one of her unblinking eyes. Taylor brought himself to brush his hand across her face, closing her eyes, and turned toward the open window. Fear jumped up in his chest. The Reverend was lurking somewhere outside and Taylor had become an unfriendly witness to murder. He quickly formulated a plan: make the Reverend believe they were still a team, head back to Vegas, and turn the son of a bitch over to the police at the first opportunity. Now he had only to steel himself against showing revulsion. His life might depend on it.

When the spasms in his throat stopped, he walked out of the hotel calling for the Reverend. It was unnecessary. The Reverend was right there in front, calmly going through Ramona's car. Taylor approached him. He turned and said, in a conversational tone, "Is she dead?

"Yes," Taylor said. "To hell with her. Nothing like a woman for causing trouble between friends. Where's the money?"

"She just might have been telling the truth about that money. I can't find any more. One way or the other, it was a pleasure shooting her."

Taylor fought back nausea as he tried to look the Reverend in the eye. He needed to maintain this pose at any cost, because as they stood there facing each other they both carried pistols in their right hands. Taylor was holding the .38. The Reverend had gotten the twenty-two out of the truck.

"Why are you holding the gun, Reverend?"

A smile flickered on the Reverend's lips. "Oh, just in case you're a little ruffled about your girlfriend's untimely end—and I might ask you the same thing." He nodded at Taylor's pistol.

Taylor glanced down briefly at the gun but responded only to what the Reverend had said to begin with: "I didn't think shooting her was a good idea. I still don't, but it's done. Maybe she did have it coming. Anyway, you and I are partners."

The Reverend snorted. "You're the kind of partner who takes the money and runs off with your partner's young stuff. And expects him to believe you were going to leave him a stake. And, uh, let me ask you this, buddy: why are you *still* holding that gun? I think you better drop it before you get hurt."

Both pistols remained pointed at the ground, but Taylor was watching the Reverend's arm as if it was a snake.

"You never cared about Stormy to begin with, Reverend. Remember? And I was going to leave you a stake. I've just got this gun in my hand because that's where it ended up. Be more than happy to drop it. I just need to know that you've calmed down."

"Sure you were gonna leave me a stake, *partner*"—he drew out the word sardonically—"sure you were gonna leave me a potful of money."

The Reverend wasn't buying it. And that could mean only one thing. Taylor actually started to drop his gun to try to put an end to this. Then he thought of what the Reverend had just done to Ramona. He tightened his grip. Desperate, he moved beside the Reverend, leaned against the car and looked into the sky. He needed to think of something that would renew a connection.

"When the gangbangers were coming into my cell, Reverend, why did you help me? I haven't seen but a couple of acts of real courage in my life. That was one."

"Could have been courage, Taylor, could have been. Or it could have been that I just wanted to mix it up with the bastards. But you ask a good question, because it's something I've been thinking about while I was out here and you were in there. Do you know what would have happened if I hadn't helped you?"

Taylor considered the prospect silently for a long moment and the Reverend answered his own question: "They would have beaten you to death."

Taylor knew it was true, but the Reverend's tone hurt his pride. "So what?" he said. "What's your point?"

"The point is that I saved your life, buddy. And as I was wondering why I did that, while I was out here trying to get us some money and you were in there trying to save a two-timing bitch that double-crossed not just you but me too, it came to me. I know exactly why I kept those bastards from killing you."

"Why?"

"Because you're mine."

Taylor was silent, struggling to accept a meaning that simply would not come. The Reverend continued, "God brought us together and led us to this moment. I can't let you leave here because I know you'll turn me in. You don't have the stomach not to. And you don't have the balls to fight me. You're going to stand there trying to appeal to my sense of empathy or compassion or whatever and I'm going to kill you."

Taylor's blood went cold, but he did have one last appeal: "This God that brought us together, doesn't this God have something to do with love and mercy?"

The Reverend gazed at the steely mountains on the horizon. "Nothing at all," he said. "Anyone who believes that God's creation reflects love, of all things, is willing his own stupidity."

Something came to Taylor which in his farthest flight of fancy he could never have imagined deciding. Right now he needed to keep talking, keep the Reverend's mind occupied.

"You're right about that, Reverend. The miraculous thing at the heart of chaos, whatever it is, the thing that generates order, that makes the sun rise and the cards fall the way they do, can't be said to have emotions at all. And you're right about something else too."

"What's that?" the Reverend asked.

"'*¿Quien es?*' might be a better question, Reverend. I am yours." The Reverend, perplexed, rolled his eyes at the serene, indifferent sky and didn't bother to look at Taylor. He rested his gaze on that point on the horizon where the sky met the distant mountains.

Taylor raised the pistol and without hesitation shot the Reverend in the head. He was dead standing up, before his knees buckled and he pitched headlong in the dust. Taylor looked down at him and said, "I'm your death."

Taylor kicked the body. "Murdering bastard," he said. The Reverend had thought he should have been born in the old west. But he didn't know much about it. Not enough anyway. He didn't know the last words of Billy the Kid.

Taylor sat down on the boardwalk, tried to ignore the motionless thing that lay before him in the street, tried to forget the other that lay inside the hotel. An hour passed as he sat there, stunned, nearly as motionless as the others. It was so entirely senseless that he felt like he was losing his mind trying to make sense of it. How could he not have seen that the Reverend was capable of something like this?

Ramona knew it from the start. And all the while that he had thought he was writing Ramona into his script, she had been writing him. Betrayal and revenge. That was what she was about. And she had created him. Betrayer. But she had wanted to live it out, replay the story with another man, and another, over and over again all the long days of her life. Like a compulsive gambler, she wanted to lose, but she didn't want to tap out and make it impossible to reenact the next loss. She didn't want to die to convince herself that her story was true.

As he sat there in a facade of a town in the middle of nowhere, something other than grief and revulsion kept crowding in. He felt like it had all been plotted. He felt like a character in a novel, that nothing that had happened to him since he played his first hand of blackjack had been under his control. It was strange, because wasn't that exactly what trying to beat a gambling game was—an attempt to control the uncontrollable? But if it all seemed plotted to lead him to this point—the deadly seriousness of which was just beginning to sink in, and which no existential "choice" could completely account for—who was doing the writing?

He couldn't think straight. He kept willing himself to be logical, to keep his emotions and his desire for absolution out of his mind, but it was hard. While he was trying to pursue a line of thought, he kept hearing Ramona asking him to hold her, seeing the light go out of her eyes.

He considered his options. The first thing that came to mind was to get into the truck, drive back to Vegas, and tell the police exactly what had happened. Then, once everything had been sorted out, he would return to Memphis, go back to his wife, and try to recover the life that he had led not so long ago.

His mind kept recoiling from this plan like flickering moments from a black-out drunk will nearly surface into consciousness, then sink again into the darkness of the night before. He finally brought it into awareness long enough to examine it, and it didn't look good. In the first place, telling the police the truth meant admitting to the plot to cheat the casino. He wasn't sure whether the fact that he had been unsuccessful, and had himself been cheated, would mitigate his criminal intent. Cheating at a blackjack table was taken very seriously in Las Vegas. In the second place, that was the least of his problems.

There had been three people out here in the desert. Two of them were dead. Who was to say that the one still alive was not the one who had killed both of the others? As Taylor thought it through, it made perfect sense that the police would believe he did exactly that . . . the only thing that would give them pause would be the fact that he had turned himself in to tell the story. That would predispose them in his favor, probably, but it wouldn't warrant a pat on the back and a free ride to Memphis. There were two gunshot bodies lying here. Somebody had to go to jail. Somebody like an ex-con who had just done time down south.

So what if he tried to lie about the Reverend and his own connection to Ramona? He couldn't begin to fabricate anything that sounded plausible. A random act? Oh yeah, by all means. He had been innocently riding along when his partner took a strange woman hostage, killed her, and then forced Taylor to defend himself. As he thought about any attempt to deny his familiarity with Ramona, a sudden thought made his blood turn cold: the casino films. The police would run back the tapes once they identified Ramona and found out where she had been working. The Reverend would not even be in the picture. Taylor would be, though, staring in disbelief at the bitch dealer who had just beaten him out of fifty thousand dollars.

Even worse, as the cops and casino personnel looked at the tapes, somebody might catch something. Taylor could imagine one of the older guys in surveillance, someone who had been around a long time, watching the tape, suddenly leaning forward just a bit, saying, "Hey, back that up and run it again." The detectives would watch the section of tape and then look perplexed toward the old man, who had seen something that someone unfamiliar with the level of expertise that can be reached with cards would find hard to imagine. Now the old man instructs them to replay the tape shot with the camera that angles in on the shuffle from behind the dealer. "Look closely and you'll see the three of diamonds fall on the ace of spades. See? Right there." And he freezes the frame. "OK, now watch the cut."

Taylor picks up the yellow card and puts it right about where the two cards are. If he cuts just above them, they will appear in the first hand or two. If he cuts just below them, they will never be dealt. On the second hand, he hits with the three of diamonds, then hits again to bust with a ten. "OK," the old man says, "that three and the ace are no longer together. The only way to explain that is that the cut card went between them and the ace is now on the bottom. But fast forward three or four hands . . . there it is." Ramona hits to twenty one with the ace of spades. "OK, back up now, and slow it down. Way down." They do and see nothing. "Give me the overhead and a zoom."

A technician fiddles with the machine, zooms in on Ramona's hands. "OK, now, run it as slow as you can. One still picture after another if we can't see it any other way, because it's there." Ramona's thumb moves over the top of the cards, seemingly pushing the top one out, but it is the bottom card that slowly, slowly is drawn into her right hand. "She was cheating him," the old man says. "Maybe he knew it too."

So now Taylor realized that the authorities might be able to find out that the body lying in the hotel was the body, in Taylor's mind, of a cheating dealer. The man with his head blown off lying in the dirt? The body of a witness to the crime. Maybe a boyfriend who was riding with Ramona.

Taylor was in deep. Nearly anyone who has been in the blackjack pits for a certain number of years can tell gambling stories all night long. Remember the one about Johnny Long, the crap shooter? Johnny was a house painter in Vegas and the casinos had taken all of what he had to begin with and what little he managed to scrape together for several years. Then one night at the Mirage Johnny won 990,000 dollars on the crap table. At dawn he quit, said he was tired, wanted to change his clothes.

The casino personnel said they would give him some clothes. He said he wanted his own. They said they would fly him home in a helicopter. They did, and then they brought him back. By noon Johnny had lost it all. The supervisors did have the decency to give the man a room, which was where he cut his wrists and humiliated himself still further by not dying.

Then there's the one about the million dollar blackjack hand. The Stardust used to boast that there was no limit on their tables as long as—what a surprise—the player did not vary his bet. A well-dressed man came in and announced that he wanted to bet one million dollars cash on a single hand. The floor supervisors gathered around as he counted out the cash and placed it more or less on top of the betting circle. The dealer shuffled and dealt. The man looked at sixteen against a ten. He chose to stand, which is easy to sneer at if you don't have a million dollar bet out in front. The dealer turned over twenty. The man didn't blink, they say, just asked to see the next card as his money was being carried away. It was, of course, a five. He got up from the table with a certain casualness, went out to the parking lot, got into his car and shot himself in the head. Taylor loved this story. The man had bet his life, and had lost with dignity.

Then there was the one about Chicago Pete, a small-time bookie and gambler who used to take the junkets to Vegas regularly when it was the only place to play. On one of these trips Pete won a quarter of a million dollars at the blackjack table. He went back home and did something smart: he invested the money in a bar. The bar was successful and Pete stayed rich for a while. But fate had something else in store. He became a drunk and within a couple of years lost the bar, wound up penniless on the street, and he stayed there until . . . he won the lottery. If he had an extra dollar that didn't go for vodka or wine, he bought a lottery ticket. And he won it. Won a ten million dollar lottery, which was more than even Pete could drink or piss away. But he wasn't about that anymore. He joined A. A., stayed sober, and died years later rich and happy.

The only way Taylor could have liked this one better would have been if Pete had won the money the second time at the blackjack table. But there was something about it that resonated, something beyond the extremes of good and bad luck. It came to him that when Pete was on the street, without a friend in the world, that he was in it so deep that he *had to keep playing.* And now Taylor understood that feeling. He was going to have to play this out. He was going to have to try to get away with two "murders," one of which was self-defense, one of which he did not commit.

The thought did occur to him to go home to his wife and tell her what had happened—but he immediately knew that that was out of the question. She would insist that he take it to the law, and if he did not, she would. The moment he realized this he felt entirely alone. Under no circumstances, ever, could he tell anyone what had happened out here. Thus, there would never again be the possibility that anyone would really know the facts of his life, really know him. From now on, he would be hiding.

Shadows were lengthening in the desert twilight. The cool dark night was coming on. Taylor knew what he had to do. When he stood up he was stiff, and he realized he had been sitting motionless for hours.

The Reverend was lying face down. Taylor took his wallet out of his pants and pocketed the thirty-three hundred. He then rolled the body over, took a leg under each arm, and began dragging him by his boots down the street. After half a block, the smattering of red bone and brain played out in the dust. Taylor pulled him around the corner and out to the mine shaft. He wrestled him inside and set him against the far wall beside the mannequin.

Now came something harder. He went into the hotel and back to the room where Ramona lay. He was going to pick her up and cradle her in his arms, but rigor mortis had begun to set in and her legs were like wood. He managed to bend her a little at the waist and picked her up over his shoulder. He took her to the mine and set her on the other side of the mannequin. She had never wanted to be around the Reverend and now they would be here forever. At least the mannequin separated them.

Taylor walked out without looking back and went to the rental car. The keys were . . . he would have to go back to the mine. As he turned into the shaft the last rays of the sun behind him illuminated the far wall and cast his huge shadow over the three figures there. It was the last light that would ever fall on them. Other than the blood all over her, Ramona didn't look hideous, just like someone asleep in an uncomfortable position. Her expression was almost sweet, as he had sometimes seen her when she was sleeping and had found himself wondering why she couldn't look like that when she was awake, why she had to face the world with a scowl. She had really never let down her guard with him. When he considered how early the computer exchanges had started, he understood why. Now she was dead. Of the three miracles, two of them were gone. The world, such as it was, remained.

Taylor fished the rental car keys out of the Reverend's pocket. He returned to the car and opened the trunk. Just as he had hoped, Ramona had also had the foresight to bring along a can of gas, which he emptied into the truck along with the ten gallons the Reverend had bought. He had been watching the gauge during the last part of the trip to this town; without this extra gas he could not have made it back to the highway, let alone the nearest gas station.

Taylor then went back to the rental car, started it, and drove into the mine. The shaft was tight on the sides but deep enough. He eased the car forward until it nearly nudged the bodies, then turned it off and squeezed out of the door. Standing just outside the mine, he took off his bloody clothes and tossed them inside. He walked back to the truck naked. Rubbing the dried blood off his hands with sand, he pulled a pair of jeans and a tee-shirt from a paper bag in the truck bed and put them on. Then he got inside the truck and drove toward the mine.

The opening of the shaft was supported by three beams in a post and lintel construction. Revving up the truck, he jammed it into gear and drove head on into the first post. The post fell backwards into the mine shaft. The lintel sagged but did not fall. He backed up and faced the second post, then decided his angle was too direct, backed up again and repositioned the truck. Best to hit it a glancing blow and keep moving out of the way. He put the truck in low gear, floored it, and caught the post with the left tip of the bumper. The post flew end over end, and from the corner of his eye he saw the lintel drop like a stone. In the side-view mirror, he watched the shaft collapse on itself. When the dust cleared, there was nothing but a hillside.

Taylor spent half an hour driving the truck on and off the hill, packing down the sandy dirt, trying not to think of what was beneath him. When he was through there was nothing to indicate that there had ever been a mine shaft there, nothing at all really, and the lack of anything growing on the hillside didn't look that different from the desert that surrounded it. Soon enough a cactus or two would start to grow, no doubt, and maybe a tumbleweed would get tangled up and take root. And there were desert flowers in their season, rare things with blooms so vivid they were bright in moonlight.

It was time to go. He considered heading toward Memphis for no other reason than that was where he had come from. There was nothing left for him there, but there was nothing anywhere else either. He took a last look at the hillside, then drove slowly out of town on the main street. Forty-five minutes later, as he approached the highway, he turned the truck lights off just in case there was someone passing. He drove by moonlight for a while, then turned onto the highway and turned his lights back on. Now no one could possibly know where he had come from.

He drove for a couple of hours without seeing a single sign of another human being, and then in the distance saw lights. Gradually, the lights got brighter and eventually he entered the town of Ely, Nevada, pop. 10,000. He saw smatterings of neon here and there, oriental red and lilac against the night sky. Enough neon to stand out in the desert, he supposed, but not much really. Nothing blazed. This was a little town. He passed a couple of "gentlemen's ranches," then saw two reasonably sized casinos on either side of the road. One of them had "Single Deck Blackjack" in bold black letters on the marquis.

Taylor pulled the truck over into a small park. He leaned back and lit a cigarette, watching the smoke rise, form patterns, then break apart. What were his options? He looked down the street at the casino entrance and felt something he had never felt before when it came to the game: fear. What was the matter with him? He had more than three thousand dollars, enough to keep him playing until the cards turned if they were bad to begin with. He could stay here, in Ely, Nevada, and finish whatever it was he had started.

It had been years since he had been here. Ely was like a town in another country, another time, something probably most Americans are not even aware exists. There were no rose-covered picket fences here. There were two whore houses, two casinos, and drunken cowboys and gamblers in the street on Saturday night. Here, he could find a permanent seat at a table with a dealer he liked, someone he could trust. He could dig in here, get a little place, make a home for himself.

It was a long way from any home he had ever imagined. Trying to relax, he eased back in the truck seat and looked at the full moon, then closed his eyes. He thought of the day he and Stormy had gone swimming in his aunt's pool, and the feeling he had had that something was about to come into focus, the thing that makes our choices turn out as they do, our half-blind choices, made as if we are looking at a dealer's down card, and whether right or wrong knowable only in retrospect. What was the phrase?—the "algorithm at the heart of chaos." Its signs were everywhere, but it had not yet shown itself.

He sat there thinking all night long. What had he lost?—his wife, his house, his job, his money. These things, though, could conceivably be replaced, the loss undone. What he could never undo were the two bodies he would carry in his head for the rest of his life, especially Ramona's. It came to him again that he could never know the simple but profound pleasure of letting someone know him completely, all that he had been and done. The family, the home with the yellow light?—just a dream that would fade in the dawn. A house of cards. When the sun rose he got out of the truck and walked toward the casino.

Printed in the United States
79533LV00004BB/7-21

9 781583 851609